S0-AGO-062

# The Three Musketeers

A Novel by Todd Strasser
Based on the Motion Picture from Walt Disney Pictures
In association with Caravan Pictures
Executive Producers Jordan Kerner and Jon Avnet
Based on the Screenplay by David Loughery
Produced by Joe Roth and Roger Birnbaum
Directed by Stephen Herek

DISNEY PRESS

NEW YORK

Copyright © 1993 by Disney Press.
All rights reserved.
No part of this book may be used
or reproduced in any manner without
the written permission of the publisher.
Printed and bound in the United States of America.
For information address Disney Press,
114 Fifth Avenue, New York, New York 10011.

FIRST EDITION

1 3 5 7 9 10 8 6 4 2

Library of Congress Catalog Card Number: 93-71247
ISBN: 1-56282-590-9

To Sam and Charlie Roberts

# PROLOGUE

*Paris, 1625*

TOWERING OVER THE HEART of the city was the Bastille, the most dreaded prison in all Europe. Deep beneath its high stone walls was a maze of dark, mysterious caverns lit by torches and filled with murky, mist-covered water. With no more sound than the quiet splashing of its oars, a boat made its way through one of these caverns. Standing in the boat was Cardinal Richelieu, a tall, menacing-looking man cloaked in red. Richelieu was the trusted adviser of the young and inexperienced King Louis XIII, though there were some who whispered that Louis's trust in the cardinal might be misplaced. For Richelieu was known as a cruel and ruthless man who would stop at nothing to achieve his own ends—whatever they might be.

When the boat came to a stop beside a stone walk-way, the cardinal stepped off and was met by half a

· 1 ·

dozen prison guards. With his long crimson robes swirling about him like clouds of blood, he started down a dark corridor. The musty air stank of unwashed bodies and spoiled food. Shrieks of torment filled the air, and large rats skittered away through the shadows.

The cardinal stopped in front of an iron door, then opened it and went into a cell. Inside, a gaunt man dressed in rags hung by rusty chains from a wall.

"Cardinal Richelieu!" The prisoner's eyes went wide with fear.

Another man stepped out of the shadows of the cell. He was dressed in black, and a black patch covered his left eye. A highly polished sword glinted at his side.

"Count de Rochefort," Cardinal Richelieu said. "What is this peasant charged with?"

"He broke into a carriage and stole some food," Rochefort replied.

"I was hungry," the peasant gasped. "My family hadn't eaten in four days. Please, in the name of God, I beg you."

Cardinal Richelieu gave Rochefort a short nod. "Very well. In the name of God."

Rochefort quietly drew his sword as the cardinal turned away. The sword flashed through the dark. The peasant screamed once and was silent.

"One less mouth to feed," the cardinal muttered as he walked away without a backward glance.

# 1

AT DAWN THE SKY was pale blue. The sun had just begun to appear over a wooded hill, and a silvery dew still covered the fields. In the distance a rooster crowed.

Suddenly the sound of clashing swords broke the silence. In a field behind a farmhouse with a thatched roof, two young men dueled fiercely. One was short and stocky, with a red, angry face. His name was Girard.

His opponent was taller, with dark hair and piercing blue eyes. His name was d'Artagnan. His lips were parted in a brilliant smile as he fought skillfully, wearing the clumsy Girard down.

Suddenly Girard slipped and fell into a puddle of mud.

"You're getting sloppy," d'Artagnan said with a laugh. "Do yourself a favor and surrender."

· 3 ·

"Never!" Girard shouted as he struggled to his feet. "My sister's honor is at stake."

"How many times do I have to tell you?" d'Artagnan asked as they began to duel again. "Nothing happened. I was merely helping her get dressed."

"Liar!" Girard shouted, lunging awkwardly at d'Artagnan, who easily sidestepped the attack. The distant rooster crowed again.

"I'm sorry, but I can't continue our duel," d'Artagnan said apologetically. "If I'm not home before my mother gets up, she'll kill me. Please surrender, Girard."

"I'd rather die first!" Girard shouted.

"Suit yourself," d'Artagnan said with a sigh. He had no intention of killing Girard, but he realized he would have to wound him to end the duel. With a quick parry d'Artagnan gave his opponent's fleshy belly a deep nick.

"Ugh!" Girard groaned, and fell to his knees. His tunic began to turn red where d'Artagnan had struck him. "My brothers will avenge me!"

No sooner were the words out of his mouth than they heard the sound of hoofbeats in the distance. Spinning around, d'Artagnan saw five horsemen galloping toward him.

"Don't tell me those are your brothers," he said.

"They are," Girard said.

"That was fast."

D'Artagnan turned and whistled for his horse. But

when the young swordsman jumped on, the brown horse began rearing and bucking wildly.

"Oh, come on!" d'Artagnan shouted. "Not now!"

Finally, he managed to bring the horse under control, and they raced away, pursued by Girard's five angry brothers.

D'Artagnan galloped through a small village, scattering peasants left and right. A vendor pulling a cart blocked his way, and d'Artagnan's horse leapt over it. Behind him one of Girard's brothers crashed into it.

One down, four to go, d'Artagnan thought.

He raced into a forest, then pulled a tree branch forward and let it swing back, knocking two more of his pursuers from their mounts. The fourth brother missed a jump, and the fifth was knocked off his horse when it galloped under a low bridge.

Finally d'Artagnan pulled on the reins and looked back at the men lying scattered on the ground behind him. One of Girard's brothers shook a fist at him.

"We'll get you, d'Artagnan!" he shouted angrily.

"I look forward to it!" d'Artagnan shouted back with glee.

He turned his horse and continued on. The sun was up—he would have to hurry to make it home before his mother awakened. She hated it when her son went out dueling before breakfast.

D'Artagnan galloped toward a stately stone house on the outskirts of the village. He dared not use the front door for fear his mother would hear him. Instead, he rode around to the back wall, dismounted, and climbed up the stone chimney. A moment later he slipped through the open window to his bedroom. He sat down in a wooden chair and began to pull off his muddy boots.

The door opened. D'Artagnan quickly hid his boots behind the chair. His mother came in, wearing a robe. She looked surprised.

"You're up?" she said.

"I couldn't sleep," d'Artagnan replied.

"Yes. Today's the day," his mother said a bit sadly. "Come with me."

D'Artagnan got up and followed his mother out to the barn behind the house. She pushed open the door, and they stepped inside. The only light came through a single window high in the wall.

"Your father was a proud man," d'Artagnan's mother said. "I never knew one as brave or as kind. He knew that his strength was a gift to be given in honor. That is why he dedicated his life to serving his king and his country. And that is why he gave his life."

She stopped beside an old trunk and pulled it open. Inside, d'Artagnan saw a torn blue-and-gold tunic, a pair of battered spurs, and a piece of white parchment bearing the words All for One and One for All.

The motto of the King's Musketeers, d'Artagnan thought.

"You have your father's heart," his mother said, kneeling before the trunk. "You have his will to fight and his courage. But these gifts have no value unless they are given in service."

She reached into the trunk and drew out a beautifully etched sword.

"It is time for you to find your fortune," she said, handing the sword to her son. "In Paris, with the King's Musketeers. This is your father's sword. Forged in the Crusades and handed down from generation to generation."

"And now to me," d'Artagnan whispered in awe, gazing down at the sword in his hands.

*   *   *

Later, after a hearty breakfast, d'Artagnan and his mother walked out to the field behind the manor house.

"Never forget the code of the d'Artagnans," his mother said.

"Always seek out adventure," d'Artagnan began.

"Never run from a fight," his mother continued. "And never submit to insults, except from the king."

D'Artagnan stared out at the broad fields of golden wheat and green grass that stretched away toward the horizon on all sides. Suddenly he felt nervous about what lay ahead.

"Uh, maybe I should wait," he said hesitantly. "Until after the harvest."

· 7 ·

"You've heard that every man in the Musketeers is on the run from something?" his mother asked with a knowing smile.

D'Artagnan nodded. "What am I running from?"

"A shrew of a mother and a drafty old house," his mother said with a chuckle. She reached up and touched his cheek in a gesture of farewell. "Now go!"

D'Artagnan gathered up his courage and jumped onto his horse. The horse bucked and skittered in a circle as d'Artagnan struggled for the reins.

"And for heaven's sake, practice your horsemanship!" his mother shouted.

"Yes, Mother." D'Artagnan waved, then dug his spurs into the horse's sides and galloped away across the fields, leaving his mother behind.

"Good luck, my son," she whispered softly, wiping a tear from her eye.

## 2

IN PARIS, the Count de Rochefort stood on a balcony overlooking a vast stone courtyard. Below him a hundred men with grim faces pulled off their blue-and-gold tunics and threw them into a pile.

"By joint edict of His Majesty King Louis the thirteenth and His Eminence Cardinal Richelieu, the King's Musketeers are officially disbanded," Rochefort proclaimed. "In preparation for the coming war with England, you men will join the infantry. Until then, you are to return to your homes and wait."

The Musketeers stared up at him with hatred and loathing in their eyes. "And who will protect the king?" one of them shouted.

"The Cardinal's Guards will take that responsibility," Rochefort replied.

Several men laughed bitterly. Others muttered and

· 9 ·

cursed. Rochefort knew they hated him, but he didn't care.

"You are hereby ordered to disperse," he shouted. "Should any of you resist, you will be arrested and imprisoned."

For a moment no one moved. Rochefort felt a tremor of fear. But then, one by one, the former Musketeers lowered their heads and left the courtyard.

Rochefort heard the sound of footsteps behind him. He turned and saw Cardinal Richelieu standing there in his red cape.

"Have all the Musketeers been accounted for?" the cardinal asked.

"All but three," Rochefort replied. "They would not surrender."

The cardinal frowned. "Our situation is most precarious. You must not allow these rebels to get in our way."

"I've sent a patrol to find them, but they haven't returned yet," Rochefort said.

"I want those men, not excuses!" the cardinal snapped angrily.

Rochefort swallowed. "We'll have them by nightfall, Your Eminence. You have my word."

*     *     *

Nearby, a lieutenant named Jussac led a regiment of the Cardinal's Guards down a street strewn with litter and inhabited by beggars. The Guards all wore red-and-gold tunics.

They came to a tavern with cracked windows and broken shutters. The tavern door opened, and two men wearing only their underwear were hurled out into the street. As the men staggered to their feet Jussac saw that both of them had bloody noses and blackened eyes. The lieutenant gasped as he realized they were members of the patrol Rochefort had sent to find the missing Musketeers.

A window on the second floor of the tavern opened, and a huge man wearing the blue-and-gold tunic of a Musketeer leaned out. His name was Porthos, and he held yet another of the Cardinal's Guards by his feet.

"Release that man!" Jussac shouted.

"With pleasure," Porthos replied, and let go.

Thunk! The helpless Guard fell to the street and lay there in a heap.

Jussac's face turned red. With an angry gesture he quickly led his men into the tavern. Inside, the place was a shambles. Tables had been overturned and chairs smashed. At one table half a dozen men in their underwear were tied to chairs. All of them were bleeding and bruised. At the head of the table sat two more Musketeers. The more handsome of the two was named Aramis; the other was Athos. Both wore wide-brimmed felt hats with feathers on them, capes, and tall leather boots with silver spurs.

Athos was wrapping a handkerchief around an ugly gash on his arm. The white fabric was quickly turning a deep red, as blood seeped through it.

"What is the meaning of this?" Jussac demanded angrily.

The lines in Athos's wise face deepened. "It's a private party celebrating the demise of the King's Musketeers. Go away."

"Athos, is that any way to treat our guests?" Aramis scolded his friend. He rose to his feet and bowed to the Cardinal's Guards. "Please come in. Your fellow Guards have been expecting you."

Jussac was not amused. "Count de Rochefort demands your presence at Musketeer headquarters."

"These gentlemen made a similar request," Athos replied, gesturing to the bound Guards seated around the table.

"Will you come peacefully?" Jussac asked. "Or at the ends of our swords?"

"What do you think, Aramis?" Athos asked, leaning back in his chair.

"Let's ask Porthos," Aramis replied, pointing upward.

Jussac looked up. He was startled to see the huge Musketeer standing on the second-floor balcony, holding on to the large wagon-wheel chandelier.

"I'll be right down!" Porthos shouted. He jumped from the balcony and swung down on the chandelier, which broke from its chain under his weight.

"Look out!" Jussac shouted to his men. But it was too late. The chandelier smashed into the Guards. Only Jussac was spared. He watched in disbelief as Porthos stood up and dusted himself off.

"The party must be over," Athos said, getting up. "Come, gentlemen, let's go see what has transpired at Musketeer headquarters." The three Musketeers walked past the fuming Jussac and left the tavern together.

A short time later they arrived at their headquarters and found the pile of blue-and-gold tunics in the empty courtyard.

"Where are our fellow Musketeers?" Porthos asked.

"They have been disbanded," a voice replied. The Musketeers turned to find the forbidding figure of Count de Rochefort looking down at them from a balcony.

"I'm trying to remember the last time I saw you in this courtyard," Athos said. "It was the day you were thrown out of the Musketeers."

"The charge was conduct unbecoming a Musketeer, if I recall correctly," added Aramis.

"You ought to know," Rochefort replied. "You three were the witnesses against me."

"It was the least we could do," Porthos said.

Rochefort gritted his teeth. "You are hereby ordered to surrender your tunics and make yourself available for the king's army."

"And if we refuse?" Aramis asked.

"Are you refusing to serve the king?" Rochefort asked.

"We are refusing to serve the cardinal," Aramis replied.

· 13 ·

"Tell the cardinal that we will continue to perform our sworn duty to protect the king," Athos said. "From enemies across the sea, *and* from traitors who sit at his right hand. Maybe he can take away our tunics, but he can't stop us from being Musketeers."

"Then consider yourselves outlaws," Rochefort snapped, and disappeared from the balcony.

Porthos glanced at the other Musketeers. "If we're going to be outlaws, I suppose we'll have to get our affairs in order."

"We'll meet at sundown," said Athos. "To celebrate. And plan our new lives."

The three friends joined hands.

"Outlaws," said Porthos.

"Citizens of France," said Aramis.

"The three Musketeers!" Athos exclaimed.

# 3

D'ARTAGNAN RODE ALL MORNING on the road that led to Paris. In the middle of the afternoon he reached the top of a hill and stopped. Across the fields in the distance he could see the steeples and towers of Paris. D'Artagnan was filled with excitement. He was on his own at last, following in his father's footsteps. He had dreamed of this for a long time—serving his king, dueling other men, and saving damsels in distress.

The sudden thunder of hoofbeats shattered the quiet. D'Artagnan turned and saw two young women on horseback galloping toward him, pursued by two horsemen. Damsels in distress! In a flash the women were past him. D'Artagnan looked up and saw a large tree branch hanging over the road. He grabbed it and pulled himself up. As the two men approached, d'Ar-

· 15 ·

jumped down from the branch, knocking one  onto the ground.

The second rider stopped, drew his sword, and charged back. D'Artagnan jumped out of the way, grabbed the man's arm, and yanked him off his horse. Both men lay still on the ground, stunned.

D'Artagnan was brushing off his hands when he saw the two women riding back toward him. They were both beautiful and dressed in the clothes of nobility. One had dark hair; the other's hair was auburn. The auburn-haired woman drew a pistol and aimed it at him.

"Do you have any idea what you've done?" she asked.

"I saved you and your friend from these bandits," d'Artagnan replied, puzzled as to why she held the gun on him. The dark-haired woman stared down at the two men lying on the ground, then laughed and rode off.

"We are not in need of saving," the auburn-haired woman said.

"That is clear to me as I stare into the muzzle of your pistol," d'Artagnan replied.

"These 'bandits' are the queen's own bodyguards," the woman said as she put the pistol away.

"Queen Anne?" d'Artagnan gasped, staring down the road after the dark-haired woman. "I—I didn't know."

The auburn-haired woman smiled. "Do you have a name?"

"D'Artagnan."

"You're a very foolish boy, d'Artagnan," she said. "But a very handsome one, too."

D'Artagnan stared back into her sparkling eyes and felt a stirring in his heart. "Thank you," he stammered. "You, too, are very handsome . . . er, I mean, beautiful."

"If I were you, I'd make myself scarce," the young woman said. "These men are going to be very angry when they wake up."

D'Artagnan turned to the bodyguards, who were beginning to stir. While he was looking away, the auburn-haired woman secretly slipped a thin gold bracelet off her wrist and dropped it on the ground.

"Till we meet again, d'Artagnan," she called, spurring her horse.

"Wait!" d'Artagnan called after her. "You didn't tell me *your* name!"

But it was too late—she was riding away. Just then d'Artagnan noticed something on the ground. A gold bracelet! The queen must have dropped it. D'Artagnan scooped it up, mounted his horse, and rode after them.

\*     \*     \*

It wasn't long before Queen Anne and her companion, whose name was Constance, arrived at the royal palace. Stableboys took their horses, and Constance went off to attend to business, leaving the queen to walk through the castle alone.

· 17 ·

Anne entered the throne room through the tall wooden door at one end. Twin thrones stood on a raised platform at the other end of the room. On the wall near them hung a huge map of the known world.

The room was cold, and Queen Anne felt a chill pass through her body. It had been only a short time since she'd married the young French king Louis and moved to Paris from her native Austria. Anne stared up at the map and felt a great yearning to be home. She was very lonely.

"Homesick?" a voice asked. Anne turned to see that Cardinal Richelieu had entered the room.

"You surprised me, Cardinal," she said, extending her hand.

"I often have that effect on people," Richelieu replied as he kneeled and kissed her hand. "I can't imagine why. I'm really a very gentle person."

He held her hand just a little longer than necessary. Finally, Queen Anne drew her hand away.

"Austria's loss is France's gain," the cardinal said, rising to his feet.

Although Anne didn't know the cardinal very well, she knew that he was the king's most trusted adviser. So she decided to trust him herself with the concerns that had been secretly haunting her for months.

"I'm not sure the king shares your opinion," she said slowly. "I've barely spoken to him since our wedding day. When he's around me, he seems so uncertain."

"Arranged marriages can be difficult," Cardinal Richelieu replied. "Your father and I thought yours would bring Austria and France closer together."

"Perhaps countries align more swiftly than people," Queen Anne said sadly.

"What a pity," the cardinal replied with a piercing gaze. "Sometimes I think love is wasted on the young."

Behind them the doors to the throne room opened, and a servant appeared. "His Majesty, the king."

Queen Anne watched her husband enter the room in his royal robes. Although he was no older than she, the robes lent an air of maturity to his tall broad-shouldered figure. He fixed his eyes on the cardinal, not seeming to notice Anne's presence.

"Cardinal Richelieu," he said sternly. "I've been looking for you."

"Your Majesty." The cardinal bowed.

Suddenly King Louis saw his wife. "Oh, Anne," he stammered, his regal bearing seeming to falter for a moment. "I didn't know you were here."

"Would you like me to go?" Anne asked. She assumed he would, as he never seemed to want her around.

To her surprise, the king shook his head. "No, please stay," he said quickly. He turned back to the cardinal. "Who gave you permission to disband my Musketeers?"

"You approved the decision," Cardinal Richelieu replied.

"But you knew I intended to address them myself," the king said. "Those men were my personal guards. I wanted to explain the situation to them."

"We are on the brink of war with England, Your Majesty," the Cardinal explained. "The Duke of Buckingham plans to invade within a month. We'll need the Musketeers in the field if we are to win. I thought it best to act quickly."

"I will be the judge of what is best," the king snapped irritably.

For a split second, Richelieu looked surprised. He wasn't used to the king speaking with such force. Then he nodded. "Of course, Your Majesty. Please forgive me."

Queen Anne covered her mouth with her hand to hide her smile. She was glad to see the cardinal put in his place. Sometimes she got the feeling that the cardinal forgot he wasn't the ruler of France. She was glad her husband had reminded him—especially after the unsettling meeting she'd had with the cardinal prior to the king's entrance.

Richelieu left the room. Anne hesitated for a moment and then started to follow him.

"Anne?" Louis said.

She stopped. "Yes?"

"Your thoughts on this matter would interest me," the king said.

Anne felt surprised again. He'd never asked for her opinion before. "It seemed to me that you did very well on your own," she replied.

Louis gave his wife a shy smile. "Thank you," he said. "Ever since my father was killed, Cardinal Richelieu has been by my side, guiding me as well as France. But sometimes I'm not sure of him. Putting the Musketeers in the army may be wise for France, but it disturbs me. Perhaps he's right, but it's confusing."

Anne stepped closer to him. For the past three months she'd tried to get close to him without much success. Now he watched her nervously.

"A lot of things are confusing," he added.

"Follow your heart and you are sure to do the right thing," Anne replied softly.

For a second, Louis simply stared at her. Anne held her breath, hoping he would take her hand, or smile—anything to show that he cared about her as a husband should care about his wife. But suddenly he turned away, saying he had to go.

Disappointed, Anne watched him hurry out of the room.

\* \* \*

In another part of the castle Cardinal Richelieu angrily pushed open a door. Inside, Count de Rochefort was adjusting his black eye patch in a mirror.

"I want those three Musketeers found," the cardinal snapped angrily. "They must not be allowed to get to the king. He is becoming as troublesome as his father."

"He's a foolish boy," Rochefort replied.

"That foolish boy has started talking back to me,"

Cardinal Richelieu said. "Before we know it he'll begin to think he can rule France better than I can. Which is all the more reason for us to act quickly."

"And what about the queen?" Rochefort asked.

Richelieu smiled. "I have *other* plans for her."

## 4

D'ARTAGNAN RODE through the streets of Paris. He was thrilled to be in the city he'd heard so much about all his life. He'd never seen a place so big, with such impressive buildings and so many people in the streets.

He was just passing a beautiful stone house when, without warning, a man jumped on him from a window. They both tumbled to the ground.

"What the devil!" d'Artagnan gasped in surprise as he untangled himself and stood up. Little did he know that the man who'd jumped him was Aramis, the most handsome and debonair of the three Musketeers. Aramis wore a dark cape that covered his blue-and-gold Musketeer's tunic.

"Why, thank you," Aramis said, dusting himself off. "You broke my fall perfectly. But I do apologize for the inconvenience."

"Go away!" d'Artagnan snapped, pushing Aramis

roughly. The next thing he knew, Aramis had grabbed him by the collar.

"If there's one thing I can't abide, it's rudeness," Aramis said.

"*You* fell on *me!*" d'Artagnan replied indignantly.

"And I apologized for it," Aramis said.

"Your apology is not accepted," d'Artagnan said, shrugging Aramis's hand off.

Aramis glared at the impudent lad. "I hope your sword is as quick as your mouth," he said.

Suddenly d'Artagnan smiled. The man was challenging him to a duel! "Quicker," he said eagerly.

"A duel then" said Aramis. "Meet me at the ruins outside the city at one o'clock."

"I'll be there," d'Artagnan replied.

Aramis bowed and headed off. D'Artagnan was delighted at the prospect of his first duel in Paris. He turned to see that his horse had wandered away. He was about to go after it when he spotted six men on horseback riding toward him. The lead rider was heavily bandaged. It was Girard and his five brothers.

He couldn't believe it—they must have followed him all the way to Paris, seeking revenge. D'Artagnan turned toward his horse, but he realized that Girard would see him if he ran to it and tried to mount it. At that moment a carriage came around the corner. D'Artagnan quickly hopped on the side of it and ducked down so that Girard and his brothers wouldn't see him as the carriage passed.

As d'Artagnan rode along he happened to glance in the window of the carriage. Inside was a woman of remarkable beauty. Her skin was as pale as alabaster, and her lips were ruby red. Her long, curly blond hair fell in ringlets to her shoulders. She turned to d'Artagnan and smiled.

D'Artagnan smiled back. He'd never been so close to a woman so beautiful. Suddenly another face lurched into view—that of a huge, fierce-looking Asian man. The next thing d'Artagnan knew, a large hand pushed him off the carriage.

Lying in the muddy street, d'Artagnan shook his head in wonder. Paris was rougher than he'd imagined.

\* \* \*

At one o'clock Aramis rode over a bridge and into the ruins outside the city. He dismounted among the lonely columns and the crumbling walls of an abandoned monastery and looked around for the boy who'd insulted him earlier. But the boy was nowhere to be seen.

"Maybe that young buffoon had sense enough not to show up," he muttered to himself.

"The young buffoon is up here, waiting for you," d'Artagnan said, sitting on a windowsill above him. Aramis looked up at him.

"Do you plan to come down, or do I have to suffer the inconvenience of climbing up there?" Aramis asked.

"Well, I wouldn't want to put you out," d'Artagnan replied, jumping down.

Aramis looked around. "I asked two of my friends to act as seconds," he said. "Unfortunately, they are not as punctual as you." He had told Porthos and Athos to meet him there on the hour.

"That's fine," d'Artagnan said. "I'm in no hurry to kill you."

"You certainly have a generous supply of confidence," Aramis said with a smile.

"I have great belief in my ability," d'Artagnan explained. He heard hoofbeats and saw two caped men approaching on horseback. They both grinned when they saw who Aramis was to duel.

"This shouldn't take long," Porthos said as he dismounted, looking d'Artagnan over. "He's barely out of the cradle."

"What is his crime?" Athos asked.

"He needs to be taught some manners," Aramis said.

Porthos stepped closer to d'Artagnan. "He doesn't even shave yet," the big Musketeer said with a laugh.

D'Artagnan felt his face turn red. "Another word and I'll fight *you* next," he threatened Porthos.

"Feisty young man, isn't he?" Porthos commented, grinning.

"How long have you been in Paris, boy?" Athos asked.

"I arrived this morning," d'Artagnan replied. "I have come to join the Musketeers."

Porthos and Aramis began to laugh.

"What's so funny?" d'Artagnan asked.

"You haven't heard?" Athos said. "The Musketeers have been disbanded."

His words struck d'Artagnan like a sword through the heart. "But I just got here," he gasped. "How can I become a Musketeer if they've been disbanded?"

The three Musketeers glanced at each other, then back at d'Artagnan. "I'd say you've got a problem," Athos said.

"My only problem is your standing in the way of my killing your friend," d'Artagnan said.

Athos frowned in disappointment. "You still want to go through with this?"

"I am a man of honor," d'Artagnan insisted, raising his sword.

"Stand aside," Aramis said to his friends. He threw back his cape and drew his sword.

D'Artagnan's jaw dropped at the sight of the blue-and-gold tunic Aramis wore beneath the cape.

"Now what's his problem?" Athos muttered.

"You're a Musketeer!" d'Artagnan gasped. As Porthos and Athos threw back their capes, revealing their tunics as well, d'Artagnan's eyes widened. "Three Musketeers!"

"Three outlaws now," Athos said bitterly.

"This is great!" d'Artagnan cried.

"I've never seen anyone so excited about dying before," Porthos said.

Aramis and d'Artagnan raised their swords and prepared to begin the duel.

"If I win, can I be a Musketeer, too?" d'Artagnan asked.

"If you win, you might have a chance to live," Aramis replied.

They'd just begun to circle each other when the sound of approaching hoofbeats filled the air. The Musketeers turned to see Jussac and a patrol of the Cardinal's Guards galloping toward them.

"Not Jussac again," Aramis groaned.

"Only a fool would try to arrest us twice in one day," Athos muttered as the cardinal's lieutenant rode up.

"The three of you are under arrest," Jussac shouted. "The boy's of no interest to me. He's free to go."

"Give us a moment," Porthos said. He turned to his fellow Musketeers. "Interesting odds. Five of them and three of us."

"It hardly seems fair," Aramis said. "Let's give them the chance to surrender."

"Excuse me," d'Artagnan put in, "but there are *four* of us."

"This is not your fight," Athos said. "You're not a Musketeer."

"I may not wear the uniform, but I have the *heart* of a Musketeer," d'Artagnan replied.

The three Musketeers smiled. The boy amused them.

"A warrior," Porthos said with a smirk.

"A poet," said Aramis.

"Do you have a name, boy?" asked Athos.

"D'Artagnan."

The Musketeers' eyes widened. "Can he be the son of our former comrade?" Aramis gasped.

"It can't be," insisted Porthos.

"It is," said Athos, who now saw the family resemblance. He extended his hand. "Welcome, d'Artagnan. I am Athos, and this is Porthos and Aramis."

They all shook hands.

"I'm pleased to meet you," d'Artagnan said.

Jussac cleared his throat impatiently. He was rapidly growing tired of listening to these niceties. The Musketeers turned and saw that the Cardinal's Guards had drawn their swords and were prepared to fight.

"Well," Porthos said, drawing his own sword, "now that we're acquainted . . ."

"There's work to do," said Athos.

A moment later the three Musketeers and d'Artagnan were locked in mortal combat with the Cardinal's Guards. As d'Artagnan fought he stole glances at the Musketeers, admiring their swordfighting styles.

Athos fought simply and brutally, slashing and slicing away at his opponent. Aramis fought delicately, with style and grace, even though he was battling two Guards at once. Porthos fought not only with a sword but with a dagger and an ax as well. He seemed to

· 29 ·

have an almost endless supply of weapons stashed under his cape.

D'Artagnan himself fought Jussac with boundless energy, attacking the lieutenant from all sides at once.

"Stand still!" Jussac shouted at him. "How do you expect me to kill you if you keep jumping around like that?"

The battle moved through the maze of ruins. Porthos finally dropped his opponent with a Spanish bolo.

"God, I love my work!" he cried as he stared with satisfaction at the Guard at his feet.

Aramis and Athos also defeated their foes. Meanwhile, d'Artagnan had jumped up onto a high ledge from which he continued to fight the frustrated Jussac.

"Have a look at our young friend," Aramis said to the other Musketeers.

"You mean he's still alive?" Athos asked in wonder.

"Looks like he's actually enjoying himself," Porthos remarked.

Indeed d'Artagnan was, for he knew the Musketeers were watching, and he was eager to prove to them that he was a skilled swordsman. He and Jussac battled along the stone ledge. To their left was a ravine hundreds of feet deep.

"Don't lose your balance," Porthos shouted gleefully.

No sooner were the words out of his mouth than

d'Artagnan suddenly slipped on a loose rock. Waving his arms desperately for balance, he teetered on the edge of the wall. The three Musketeers watched with bated breath.

Seeing an opportunity to catch his opponent off guard, Jussac lunged forward. D'Artagnan managed to twist out of the way of Jussac's sword. At the same time, Jussac's momentum carried him past d'Artagnan and into the air beyond. A second later he had disappeared over the wall.

D'Artagnan turned to the Musketeers and grinned proudly. Porthos winked at Athos, and the two men turned away as if they were completely uninterested.

D'Artagnan climbed down from the ledge. The Cardinal's Guards lay scattered throughout the ruins. Aramis kneeled next to one of them, muttering solemnly under his breath.

"What's he doing?" d'Artagnan whispered to Athos.

"Giving the man his last rites," Athos replied. "Aramis takes death very seriously."

Porthos also kneeled next to his defeated foe, but only to retrieve his bolo. As the big Musketeer pulled open his cape, d'Artagnan saw the collection of other unusual weapons stashed there.

"I know what you're thinking," Porthos said when he noticed d'Artagnan watching him. "You're wondering why a great swordsman like myself would carry anything but a sword."

D'Artagnan nodded.

"I like the variety," Porthos said. "This bolo, for instance, was a gift from the queen of America."

"There is no queen of America," d'Artagnan corrected him.

Porthos frowned. "Boy, you are arrogant, hot-tempered, and entirely too bold!"

For a moment d'Artagnan thought the big man meant it, but then Porthos grinned.

"Don't encourage him," Aramis warned Porthos. "The boy's now made himself an outlaw, too."

"Not if he leaves Paris immediately," Athos said.

"I don't want to leave," d'Artagnan protested. "I just got here."

"Go home, boy," advised Porthos. "Find a wench. Live long and prosper."

D'Artagnan couldn't believe they were serious. "Why can't I join you?"

Aramis and Porthos glanced at Athos. D'Artagnan sensed that he was their leader.

"Because I don't want you to," Athos said simply. He and the other Musketeers mounted their horses. D'Artagnan was so disappointed he felt as if his heart might break.

Aramis could see how hurt the boy was. "This is our fight, not yours," he said. "Go on, get out of here."

"Whatever happened to the motto of the Musketeers?" d'Artagnan asked, refusing to give up. "All for One and One for All?"

· 32 ·

"Wake up, boy," Athos muttered. "The Musketeers are part of the past."

D'Artagnan watched sadly as the three Musketeers spurred their horses and rode away. Oddly, the noise their three steeds made sounded like a whole herd of horses. D'Artagnan looked around, puzzled.

There *was* a whole herd of horses! They were being ridden by a new regiment of the Cardinal's Guards. A rider in black, wearing an eye patch, led them. Ignoring d'Artagnan, the Guards rode into the ruins and found the bodies of their fallen comrades. The man in black pointed his sword at the three Musketeers, who were still in sight as they crossed a nearby field.

"There they are!" he shouted. "After them!"

Even if he couldn't be a Musketeer himself, d'Artagnan was determined to help them. He jumped on his horse and rode straight toward the Cardinal's Guards with his sword drawn.

"Long live the Musketeers!" he shouted.

Halfway across the field the three Musketeers heard d'Artagnan's cry. They stopped their horses and looked back as d'Artagnan attempted to take on all the Guards at once.

"Do you believe that kid?" Porthos asked in wonder.

"Look, it's Rochefort," Aramis said, pointing at the figure in black.

At that very moment Rochefort was waving the Guards away. "Fall back!" he shouted to them. "I'll take the boy myself."

· 33 ·

The Guards obeyed. Like medieval knights, d'Artagnan and Rochefort met in the middle of the field. Their blades clashed together violently, and d'Artagnan was thrown from his horse.

"He needs help," Aramis said.

"In time," Athos said, raising his hand to stop his friends from riding to d'Artagnan's aid.

The guards surrounded the boy while Count de Rochefort dismounted. D'Artagnan picked up his sword and jumped to his feet. But with a quick flick of his blade, Rochefort sent the boy's sword flying. D'Artagnan gasped in astonishment. He'd never seen a sword move so quickly.

Without a word Rochefort nodded to a burly Guard standing behind d'Artagnan. The boy felt a hand grab his shoulder and spin him around. Then a huge fist smashed into his face and everything went black.

# 5

D'ARTAGNAN OPENED his eyes. He was lying on a cold stone floor in a dark, foul-smelling cell. His jaw throbbed painfully, and his whole body felt stiff and sore. Suddenly he felt the tip of a sword prick his thigh. He leapt up and knocked the sword away, then reached for where his own should have been.

"My sword!" he gasped when he realized it was gone.

"It's magnificent," a voice said. D'Artagnan squinted into the shadows and saw the man with the black eye patch step out.

"Who are you?" d'Artagnan asked. "Where am I?"

"I am Count de Rochefort, captain of the Cardinal's Guards. And you are in the dungeon of the Bastille."

"The prison?" D'Artagnan's eyes went wide.

· 35 ·

"Yes," Rochefort replied. "Now, I have a question for you. Where did you get this sword?"

"It belonged to my father," d'Artagnan said proudly.

"Your father?" Rochefort's reaction was similar to that of the Musketeers earlier that day.

"Did *you* know him, too?" d'Artagnan asked.

Count de Rochefort ignored the question. "Your sword is now mine. I collect them from the men I kill."

"I'm not dead yet," d'Artagnan replied, stepping toward him. But a second later he felt the sharp point of his father's sword pressing against his throat.

"You and the Musketeers are responsible for the death of Cardinal's Guards," Rochefort said. "It is an offense punishable by death."

"But they interrupted a duel we were about to fight," d'Artagnan protested.

"Duels are also punishable by death," Rochefort replied. "However, if you tell me where to find the Musketeers, I may be lenient."

"How?" d'Artagnan asked.

"I will return your father's sword."

D'Artagnan stared at the sword as he thought it over. Then he stepped close to the count and whispered, "Give me my father's sword, and I will cut your heart out."

Rochefort gritted his teeth angrily, then suddenly slammed the sword's handle into the brash young man's head. D'Artagnan slumped to the floor.

"Idiot," Rochefort muttered. "Just like your father."

Rochefort stormed out of the cell, nodding to a grizzled jailer who waited outside.

"Shackle him," Rochefort ordered, and departed.

The jailer stepped into the cell. Without warning, d'Artagnan jumped up and hit him in the jaw as hard as he could. The jailer fell to the floor, unconscious.

A moment later d'Artagnan crept out of the cell, dressed in the jailer's clothes. Searching for a way out, he sneaked slowly down the dark, dank halls. Desperate hands reached toward him through the bars of the foul-smelling cells lining the way, but he couldn't stop. Each hallway seemed to lead to a dead end. How would he ever find his way out of this horrible place?

Suddenly he heard footsteps. Stepping into the shadows, he saw Rochefort approach, accompanied by several guards and a mysterious figure shrouded in a dark brown cloak. D'Artagnan waited until the group passed, then fell into step behind the guards.

They came to a stairway that led to a wooden door. The door opened slowly, and a tall man in a red cape stepped out.

*Cardinal Richelieu!* D'Artagnan recognized him with a start. He watched as the cardinal beckoned Rochefort and the cloaked figure through the door. The guards turned to leave, and d'Artagnan pretended to follow them. Then he doubled back and stood just outside the door. Inside, he could hear the cardinal talking to the mysterious figure.

"I have an errand that requires your singular talents," Richelieu was saying. D'Artagnan could hear the rustle of paper. "Carry this treaty to the Duke of Buckingham."

"You're making an alliance with England?" asked a woman's voice.

"The king has left me no choice," Richelieu replied. "He's begun to get too big for his crown. The boy is beginning to believe he should rule France instead of me."

"I understand," the woman replied with an evil laugh.

"You are to leave for Calais at once," the cardinal ordered. "A ship called the *Persephone* sails Tuesday at midnight. Lord Buckingham must sign the treaty before the king's birthday on Friday."

"Consider it done."

"In doing so, you shall earn the gratitude . . . of the *next* king of France," Richelieu said.

A second later d'Artagnan heard the sound of footsteps moving toward the door. He quickly backed away and joined the other jailers, who were waiting farther down the hall. Suddenly d'Artagnan felt a hand clamp down on his shoulder and spin him around. He found himself looking up into the face of Count de Rochefort.

"On your knees!" the count shouted, forcing d'Artagnan down. The young man fell to his knees. Looking up, he saw that Cardinal Richelieu had joined them.

"Who is this?" the cardinal asked.

"He was with the Musketeers who killed Jussac and the others," Rochefort replied. "I believe he was just listening behind the door."

Richelieu stared down at d'Artagnan. "How much did you hear?"

"Hardly a word," d'Artagnan lied. "The voices were much too low, with all the noise of the prison . . ."

"What is your name, boy?" Richelieu asked.

"D'Artagnan."

"Ah, yes." The cardinal nodded. "Your father was a Musketeer."

"He died protecting the king," d'Artagnan said. To his surprise, the cardinal chuckled.

"The dream of every warrior," Richelieu said. "To die nobly for king and country. But I believe you've been misled, boy. Your father died a much less noble death . . . in the arms of a woman."

"Her husband found them together," Rochefort added with a devious smile, "the night the king was assassinated."

The news stunned d'Artagnan. Could it really be true that his father had neglected his duties and allowed assassins to kill the king?

"Tell me, d'Artagnan," said the cardinal. "What noble business brings you here?"

"I came to join the King's Musketeers," d'Artagnan answered proudly.

The cardinal's eyebrows rose, and he shook his head. "Bad timing."

"So I've heard," d'Artagnan said.

"Where are your friends, the three Musketeers?" Richelieu asked.

"I can't tell you what I don't know," d'Artagnan replied.

"A pity," Cardinal Richelieu said, shaking his head. "Please give my regards to the executioner." He began to turn away.

"Wait," d'Artagnan said.

The cardinal stopped and turned. "Why? Do you object to losing your head?"

"Yes. I like it where it is."

"Then tell me what I want to know and perhaps you can keep it there a few years longer," said the cardinal.

"I don't know where they are," d'Artagnan replied. "And if I did, I wouldn't tell you."

Richelieu smirked. "I admire your courage, boy. You might have made a fine Musketeer. But we'll never know, will we?"

# 6

WITHIN A FEW HOURS d'Artagnan was led into the market square, where a crowd had gathered. With his hands bound behind his back he gazed up bravely at the scaffold where the execution would take place. Several of the Cardinal's Guards stood on the scaffold, along with a priest clad in a black cassock, his broad-brimmed hat pulled low over his face. Near him a hooded executioner ran his thumb along the razor-sharp blade of his ax.

As d'Artagnan climbed the steps toward the executioner, he gazed out at the crowd. He noticed that his enemy Girard was among them. The bandaged man had a delighted smile on his face.

Farther away, on the edge of the crowd, the queen and Constance happened to be riding past on horseback.

"Barbarism disguised as justice," Queen Anne

commented sadly when she saw what was going on.

Constance glanced at the young man on the platform and gasped. "It's him!"

"Who?" Anne asked.

"The boy who saved us from our own guards," Constance said. At that very moment d'Artagnan looked up, and their eyes met. Constance turned to the queen. "Can't you stop this cruelty?"

The queen touched her friend's hand gently. "I'm sorry. There is nothing I can do."

D'Artagnan reached the top of the platform. He stared at the bloodstained wooden block where he would soon lay his head, and swallowed fearfully. The priest and the executioner stood quietly nearby, but d'Artagnan could not see their faces. The priest took a step closer.

"Fear not, my son, for we are all with you," he said.

D'Artagnan nodded sadly. Such words could not soothe him now, not when his head was about to be cleaved from his neck.

"All for one and one for all," whispered the priest.

D'Artagnan's eyes widened as the priest slowly turned and winked at him from beneath the brim of his hat. It was Aramis!

Suddenly d'Artagnan felt the executioner grab him by the neck and push his head down onto the block. The executioner leaned close to him. "Don't worry, boy," he said quietly. "You won't feel a thing."

"Porthos!" d'Artagnan gasped in a whisper. "But where's Athos?"

No sooner were the words out of his mouth than shouts of surprise rose out of the crowd. D'Artagnan raised his head to see a crimson carriage pulled by four white stallions racing toward the platform, the crowd scattering before it. In the driver's seat, clutching the reins with one hand and cracking a whip with the other, was Athos.

Porthos instantly swung the blunt end of his ax, knocking several Guards off the scaffold. Aramis opened his Bible, pulled out a pistol, and shot another Guard. A moment later the crimson carriage pulled up below them. Athos stood up and bowed.

"Gentlemen, your carriage," he said. "Compliments of the cardinal."

The cardinal's carriage! d'Artagnan thought with giddy delight. He jumped down onto the driver's seat beside Athos. Porthos and Aramis jumped onto the top of the carriage, ripping through the fabric roof and landing in the plush interior.

All around them peasants cheered. Constance's heart soared as she watched. Near her, two of the Cardinal's Guards raced toward their horses with swords drawn. Constance quickly spurred her horse toward them, knocking both to the ground.

"Oh dear, I'm so sorry," she apologized sweetly.

As the cardinal's carriage sped away from the square, bouncing and rattling over the cobblestones,

Porthos spied a wicker basket on the floor inside. "Well, what have we here?" he commented, lifting the lid. Inside were bread, cheese, fruit, and wine. Porthos smiled at Aramis.

"How nice of the cardinal to provide us with a snack," he remarked, pulling out a bottle of wine and some bread. Aramis leaned over and took a small box out of the basket. It was filled with gold coins and jewels.

"How interesting," Aramis said. "It makes you wonder if the cardinal is a man of God—or a man of gold?"

The sound of hoofbeats caught his attention. Looking out the back of the carriage, Aramis saw a dozen of the Cardinal's Guards racing behind them on horseback. They were gaining on the carriage rapidly. Aramis reached up through the torn roof of the carriage and handed the box to d'Artagnan.

"Excuse me, boy," Aramis said. "Would you be so kind as to distribute these to the people? Your generosity will be greatly appreciated."

"But . . ." D'Artagnan hesitated.

"Throw the coins, boy," Aramis said firmly. "The people are hungry."

D'Artagnan tossed a handful of coins in the air. Peasants quickly scrambled onto the street to retrieve them, blocking the way of the Cardinal's Guards.

Bang! D'Artagnan heard a loud popping sound. He ducked down in his seat, thinking it was pistol fire.

· 44 ·

"They're firing at us!" he cried. To his amazement Porthos responded by handing a bottle of champagne through the roof to Athos. Athos took the bottle and gave the reins to d'Artagnan.

D'Artagnan's face turned red as he realized that the sound he'd heard had been caused by the popping of the bottle's cork. Athos put the bottle to his lips and took a big gulp while d'Artagnan struggled to control the carriage.

"Turn right at the next street," Athos said.

D'Artagnan instantly jerked on the reins, and the carriage careened around the corner, tipping up on two wheels. As the carriage started up a steep hill, Porthos stuck his head out of the back. His face and tunic were soaked with wine.

"Don't let the boy drive!" he shouted at Athos.

Athos finished his champagne and took back the reins. By now they'd reached the top of the hill. Athos yanked on the reins, and the carriage stopped. He jumped down and pulled open the carriage door.

"Gentlemen," Athos said to Porthos and Aramis, "this is the end of your trip. I hope you had a pleasant ride." He turned to d'Artagnan and said, "Unhitch the horses."

"But the Guards . . ." D'Artagnan pointed down the hill, where half a dozen of the Cardinal's Guards were now thundering toward them.

"Do as I say," Athos ordered. While d'Artagnan unhitched the horses, Athos tossed a sack of gunpowder into the carriage. When they were all clear, he took careful aim with his pistol and sent a bullet flying into it. The cardinal's carriage burst into flames.

Athos gave the burning carriage a shove. It started to roll down the hill toward the approaching Guards, who turned and began fleeing for their lives.

\* \* \*

The Musketeers and d'Artagnan rode for hours on the cardinal's white stallions before stopping to relax beneath some trees. D'Artagnan was glad to rest while the others finished off the last of the cardinal's picnic. He kept thinking back to how he'd just been rescued.

"I was certain my head was going to end up on the cardinal's mantel," he said.

"Your trip from home has been an eventful one," Aramis observed.

"You know," said Porthos as he gnawed on a turkey leg, "your father was a captain of the Musketeers when we were just recruits."

"A good man, I'm told," Aramis said.

"He was killed when I was a boy," d'Artagnan said sadly. "All my mother would tell me was that he died in the service of the king. But I have recently learned that he may have died under . . . different circumstances."

For a moment no one said anything. The Musketeers gave each other knowing looks. Finally, Athos spoke. "Your father was murdered," he said in a low voice.

D'Artagnan stared at him uncertainly.

"He uncovered a plot to kill the king," Athos went on. "On the way to foil the plan he and another Musketeer were ambushed outside the Louvre."

"This other Musketeer," d'Artagnan said. "Is he still alive? I'd like to talk to him."

"You already have," Porthos said. "He is Count de Rochefort."

"Rochefort?" D'Artagnan was puzzled. "But he and the cardinal are plotting against the king."

"Tell us something we don't know," Aramis said, rolling his eyes.

"I'm serious," d'Artagnan said. "I overheard them. The cardinal sent someone to England with a secret treaty for a man named Buckingham."

The Musketeers looked at each other with alarm.

"Not the *Duke* of Buckingham?" Porthos asked.

D'Artagnan nodded. "Do you know him?"

"He rules England the way Richelieu rules France," Aramis said.

"The cardinal's messenger is going to Calais," d'Artagnan said. "To meet a ship called the *Persephone*, which sails Tuesday at midnight."

Aramis rubbed his chin and stared into the distance. "Calais is over two hundred leagues from here."

"If we could get our hands on this messenger and

the treaty, it would prove once and for all that the cardinal is a traitor," Porthos said.

"Tell me, d'Artagnan," Athos said. "Does the cardinal know you have this information?"

"Yes."

"Then he knows we have it, too," Athos said. "He will do everything in his power to stop us."

"But with three men trying, one of us should be able to make it," Porthos said.

"Excuse me," d'Artagnan interrupted him. "You mean, with *four* men trying."

The Musketeers glanced at each other and *almost* smiled.

# 7

CARDINAL RICHELIEU STOOD on the roof of the palace, looking out over the silent rooftops of Paris. He was terribly angry—not just because the Musketeers had destroyed his personal carriage and escaped but because as long as they remained free, his plan to become king was in danger.

The cooing of the pigeons caught his attention. Richelieu turned to a large wooden pigeon coop and watched as servants attached messages to the legs of half a dozen pigeons. Nearby, a door swung open and Rochefort appeared, out of breath from running.

"The Musketeers have been spotted on the road to Calais," he said.

The cardinal nodded grimly. "I've put one thousand pistoles on each of their heads, dead or alive. I'm sure that by now the boy has told them of my plans."

"How will you get out the word?" Rochefort asked.

"Thanks to my winged friends," Richelieu said, gesturing at the pigeons, "soon every mercenary and bounty hunter in France will be after the Musketeers."

The cardinal signaled to the servants, who immediately sent the pigeons flying off into the air. "All for one," Richelieu muttered, "and more for me."

\* \* \*

As darkness fell, the Musketeers and d'Artagnan came across a wagon overturned in a ditch. Wooden beer kegs littered the road. The wagon's driver, an old farmer, sat on one of the kegs, holding his head in despair.

"My horse broke loose," the farmer cried as the riders approached. "Can you help me move these kegs out of the road?"

D'Artagnan started to dismount.

"Stay on your horse," Athos ordered.

"But this man needs our help," d'Artagnan said.

The words were hardly out of d'Artagnan's mouth before two more men stepped out of the woods, aiming muskets at the riders. The farmer reached into his coat and pulled out a pistol.

"Won't you please step down, Musketeers?" he said with a cruel smile.

"Gentlemen, I beg you," Aramis replied. "Please put away your weapons. We'd prefer to ride on without having to kill you."

"Are *you* threatening *us?*" the farmer asked with a haughty laugh. He raised his pistol and aimed it at Aramis.

Bang! Bang! Bang! Three shots rang out. D'Artagnan winced and shut his eyes. When he opened them, the farmer and his companions lay on the ground. Each of the three Musketeers held a smoking pistol in his hand.

"There's only one rule between here and Calais, d'Artagnan," Porthos said grimly. "Stay alive."

The four horsemen rode on. They heard thunder in the distance. Soon it began to rain, slowing their progress. After a few minutes it became clear that they would have to stop and wait out the storm. As they dismounted and headed for the door of a country inn, Athos warned the others to be cautious. With their cloaks drawn around them and the brims of their hats pulled low to cover their faces, they entered the inn.

Inside, a handful of weary travelers sat at wooden tables, and several barmaids stood by the bar. A fire roared in a stone fireplace. The innkeeper, an old, balding man wearing a stained white apron, approached the Musketeers.

"Good evening, gentlemen," he said, eyeing them nervously.

"See to our horses and bring us some food," Athos commanded.

"I'm sorry, sir," the innkeeper replied humbly.

"We have very little to spare. The Cardinal's Guards were here today. They helped themselves to my food and then refused to pay."

At that moment Porthos's cape slid off his shoulder, revealing his blue-and-gold tunic.

"Musketeers!" a barmaid gasped.

With the sound of sliding steel the three Musketeers and d'Artagnan drew their swords and stood back-to-back in a circle, ready to fight.

But no one attacked. In fact, everyone looked thrilled to see them.

"Musketeers in my inn!" the innkeeper exclaimed happily. "Gentlemen, put away your swords and sit down. Anyone who fights the cardinal is welcome here. We don't have much, but what we have is yours."

The barmaids took the men's dripping wet capes and hung them by the fire to dry. Aramis turned to his companions. "I think we've found a home," he said with a wink.

The evening turned out to be a festive one. D'Artagnan and the Musketeers ate and drank well. Porthos and Aramis took turns instructing d'Artagnan in the art of kissing barmaids. As the evening wore on, however, d'Artagnan noticed that Athos was sitting at a table by himself with a scowl on his face and a bottle of burgundy in front of him.

"Why does Athos sit off by himself like that?" d'Artagnan asked.

"He takes his drinking seriously," Aramis replied.

"In all the years I've known him, I have never seen him smile."

D'Artagnan crossed the room to where Athos sat. "Come join us," he said.

Instead, Athos pulled the boy down beside him. "You fight like a man," Athos said. "Now let's see if you can drink like one."

"I'll drink anything you put in front of me," d'Artagnan said, taking the dare.

"Famous last words," Athos said, pouring them each a glass of wine. "Now, what shall we drink to?"

D'Artagnan glanced across the room at a beautiful dark-haired barmaid. "Shall we drink to love?"

Athos grimaced as if the word caused him pain. "Love? Have *you* ever been in love?"

D'Artagnan reached into his pocket and pulled out the bracelet he'd found on the road to Paris. It reminded him of the young woman with the auburn hair. "There is a woman I can't get out of my mind."

Athos shook his head slowly. "Would you like to hear a love story?"

"Yes," replied d'Artagnan.

Athos took a long gulp of wine. "I once knew a man," he began. "His name was Count Berry. When the good count was about your age, he fell in love with a beautiful girl. No, she was *more* than beautiful. She was mysterious and intoxicating. He was consumed by her. . . . And then the poor idiot married her."

· 53 ·

"But isn't that what people do when they fall in love?" d'Artagnan asked.

"Just listen," Athos said. "The count took the girl to his castle and made her the first lady of the province. For a time they were happy. Then, while riding in the woods one day, the girl was thrown from her horse and knocked unconscious. Her dress was torn. The count hurried toward her and saw something on her shoulder that she'd kept hidden till then."

"What was it?" d'Artagnan asked.

"The mark of the fleur-de-lis. The count realized that mark meant his wife was a murderess who had escaped the executioner's blade. When she returned to health she swore that she loved him and that she had changed. She begged him to keep her secret and promised they would live a long, happy life together."

"But?" d'Artagnan said expectantly when Athos paused to take another swig.

"But the count was young and stupid," Athos said. "He not only rejected her, he turned her over to the authorities to be executed for her crimes."

Athos sighed. "It was only later that the count realized what she had meant to him and how stupid he'd been. His own betrayal was far worse than whatever she had done. Soon after that he gave up his castle and his title and disappeared forever."

"All in the name of love." D'Artagnan sighed.

"Have another drink," Athos said, pushing the bottle of wine toward him.

"I've had enough," d'Artagnan replied.

"Good." Athos pulled back the bottle. "More for me."

*    *    *

Dawn came much too quickly. Soon it was time to remount the cardinal's white stallions and continue the journey to Calais.

D'Artagnan had a pounding headache from sleeping too little and drinking too much. Every step his horse took made him wince. He had to squint in the early morning light.

"Beautiful morning, eh, d'Artagnan?" Porthos's voice boomed beside him as they rode.

"My head feels as though it's filled with dueling guardsmen," d'Artagnan moaned. "And would you please stop whistling?"

"I'm not whistling," Porthos replied.

"Well, someone is," d'Artagnan said. "And it's getting louder."

"The barmaid's kiss left him dizzy," Porthos told the other Musketeers.

"Wait," said Aramis. "Now I hear it, too."

"It's a cannonball!" Athos shouted.

Boom! The cannonball landed a dozen yards away, startling the horses and throwing clods of dirt and rocks high into the air.

Boom! Another fell even closer. The Musketeers struggled to control their frightened stallions.

"Look," Aramis shouted. "Up on the hill!"

On a hill not far away stood a castle. In front of it a group of men reloaded two rusty old cannons.

"This way!" Athos shouted as he began to spur his horse across an open field. The others followed, but a second later a group of horsemen appeared in front of them.

Athos quickly changed direction, but another group of horsemen appeared. A crossroads lay just ahead of the four friends.

"Split in half!" Athos shouted. "D'Artagnan rides with me!"

D'Artagnan galloped after Athos as Porthos and Aramis started down the other road. "See you in Calais!" Aramis shouted.

## 8

INSIDE THE ROYAL PALACE, in a room heavy with heat and steam, Queen Anne reclined in a bathtub. To keep the bathwater hot, Constance brought pitchers of steaming water from a cauldron boiling over a fire. They were talking about d'Artagnan.

"How can I know if I'm really in love?" Constance asked.

"The first time you saw him," Anne said, "did your knees feel as weak as water?"

"Yes," Constance replied with a giggle.

"And when he looked at you, did you suddenly forget how to breathe?" the young queen asked.

"Yes."

Anne's fine eyebrows arched. "Do you think about him all the time?"

Constance nodded and blushed.

"Then you're in love," Anne said with a smile.

· 57 ·

Constance smiled back. She was happy that she was in love, but worried because she had no idea where d'Artagnan was. She would have to wait for him. But in the meantime she had a question for her queen.

"Are you in love, Your Majesty?" she asked.

"What an impertinent question." Anne pretended to be shocked.

"Are you?" Constance pressed her friend.

Anne was silent for a moment. Then she said, "My love . . . is a matter of state. It's complicated."

She seemed sad. Constance knew how to make her smile. "Do you think about him all the time?"

"As queen, my mind touches on many subjects," Anne replied with mock formality.

"Do your knees feel as weak as water?" Constance asked.

"Never!" Anne insisted.

"When he looks at you, do you forget how to breathe?" Constance asked.

"I hope I will someday," Queen Anne replied wistfully. "I hope *he* will, too."

\*     \*     \*

After Anne finished her bath, Constance helped her into her robe and then left the room. A moment later Anne remembered something and followed her into the dressing chamber.

"Constance," she called, "have you seen my . . ."

Someone was in the dressing chamber, but it wasn't Constance. It was Cardinal Richelieu.

· 58 ·

"What are you doing here?" Anne asked, pulling her robe more tightly around her.

"Forgive me for intruding, Your Majesty." The cardinal bowed. "I need your help and could not in good conscience wait another minute."

"You need *my* help?" Anne asked suspiciously.

"Yes," Richelieu replied. "You see, I am worried about . . . your happiness."

"My happiness is not your concern," Anne replied.

"But it is," Richelieu insisted. "You are too occupied with problems of state. The Huguenot rebellion, the occupation in the Antilles, and the coming war with England—these are not the usual concerns of youth. I am worried that you and the king do not have enough time alone."

"We are still getting to know one another," Anne replied.

"But you are husband and wife," Richelieu pointed out.

Anne did not know why the cardinal wanted to speak of these things, but he was making her uncomfortable.

"My marriage was arranged," she said. "By *you.*"

The cardinal smiled and stepped closer. "If you are not happy with it, perhaps you should consider all that you and *I* might accomplish . . . together."

Anne stepped back, but Richelieu took a step forward and stared down into her eyes. "Never forget, Your Majesty, kings come and go," he said. "Only one thing remains the same. Me."

· 59 ·

Suddenly he turned and left the room. Anne watched him go. His words filled her with dread. Whatever Richelieu meant, she knew it did not bode well for the king.

*     *     *

From Anne's dressing chamber, the cardinal proceeded to the throne room, where King Louis stood on the balcony looking out sadly over the city.

"I'm sorry to be late, Your Majesty," Richelieu said as he joined him. "I was wrestling with an important matter of state."

King Louis studied him. "I've heard some very troubling rumors about you."

"There are so many to choose from," the cardinal replied with a cunning smile.

"Is betrayal one of them?" the king asked.

"Ah, yes," Richelieu replied with an easy laugh. "That is usually the first the new king hears. It goes something like this: While the English attack from the north, the wicked cardinal forges a secret alliance with Lord Buckingham and places himself on the throne."

King Louis nodded, caught off guard. That was *precisely* what he had heard. But if it was true, why was the cardinal so quick to admit it?

"Why stop there?" Richelieu asked. "Haven't you heard that I make oaths with pagan gods? Or that I seduce queens in their chambers and teach pigs to dance?"

King Louis smiled a little and began to relax.

Young d'Artagnan arrives in Paris, eager to follow in his late father's footsteps and join the King's Musketeers.

Count de Rochefort, henchman of the evil Cardinal Richelieu, has just ordered the Musketeers to disband.

Only three Musketeers refuse to turn in their blue-and-gold tunics–Athos, Aramis, and Porthos.

D'Artagnan meets the three rebel Musketeers and joins forces with them...

...which soon lands him in the Bastille, where the cardinal sentences him to death.

Luckily d'Artagnan's new friends don't let him down–they stage a dramatic rescue in the cardinal's own carriage!

After an exciting chase through the countryside, the four friends finally escape their pursuers. They vow to do all they can to save the king from the cardinal's treachery.

Meanwhile, the cardinal is wooing Queen Anne's favor as he secretly plots to overthrow her husband, King Louis XIII.

Discovering that Richelieu plans to have the king assassinated at his birthday celebration, the Musketeers return to Paris just in time to join the crowds heading toward the palace for the festivities.

Inside the palace, the king and queen prepare to step onto the balcony to greet the citizens of France.

The three Musketeers throw off their disguises and prepare to take on the Cardinal's Guards.

A full-scale battle rages between Musketeers and Guards, and d'Artagnan must face the man who killed his father–Count de Rochefort.

D'Artagnan and the Musketeers finally triumph over the evil cardinal and his Guards. King Louis rewards d'Artagnan by officially declaring him a Musketeer.

The four Musketeers stride through the streets of Paris–all for one and one for all!

"Now that you've put it that way, it does seem far-fetched."

"If there are any doubts about my loyalty," the cardinal said, "they'll be put to rest when we appear together at your birthday celebration."

"My birthday!" the king said. "I'd almost forgotten."

"France is eager to celebrate the birth of its king," Richelieu reminded him. "It will be a day to remember, Your Majesty."

\*   \*   \*

Porthos and Aramis rode hard. At the crossroads their pursuers had also split up, half the guards following them while the other half followed Athos and d'Artagnan. As Porthos and Aramis reached the top of a tall bluff, they could see that the guards who were chasing them had fallen some distance behind but were still coming doggedly on.

"Let's go," Porthos said impatiently.

"No, wait," Aramis gasped. "My horse will not survive another league."

"And you?" Porthos asked.

"I, too, am tired," Aramis admitted.

Porthos rode to the crest of the hill. He looked down and smiled. Below was a swift, choppy river. A large wooden raft waited on the riverbank to ferry people across. "Here's just the thing—a nice relaxing boat ride."

They rode down the hill and joined the others waiting to make the trip across the river—two armed

· 61 ·

gentlemen on horseback and a woman with a young girl. The ferryman was old and grizzled, his back hunched from years of pushing the ferry.

The armed gentlemen paid the ferryman, who then turned to the woman. "The cost of the trip is two pistoles," he said.

"I have only one," the woman said. "Can't my little girl ride for free? She's so small."

The old ferryman shook his head. "Everyone pays."

"She will ride for free," Aramis said. "Under our protection."

"Nobody rides for free," the ferryman said angrily, shaking his fist. "Under your protection, indeed! I'll teach you a thing or two about protection! Who do you think you are?"

"Musketeers," Aramis replied.

"Musketeers?" The ferryman calmed down immediately. "Why didn't you say so? Of course you'll ride for free. And so will this lady *and* her pretty little girl."

Aramis winked at Porthos, and the two Musketeers led their steeds onto the raft. No sooner had the ferryman pushed off from the riverbank than the Cardinal's Guards rode up, shouting angrily. Porthos waved at them cheerfully, knowing that the raft was already a safe distance from the shore. Then he looked around and noticed that the two gentlemen were eyeing Aramis and him.

"You must be the Musketeers everyone's been looking for," one of them said.

"Popularity has its price," Porthos replied.

"There's supposed to be quite a bounty on your heads," said the second gentleman.

"No wonder everyone's been following us," Aramis said with mock surprise. But he wasn't surprised by what happened next. The gentlemen pulled their swords.

The duel was fierce and difficult. The Musketeers not only had to defend themselves, they had to protect the woman and her child from the flashing blades. They fought up and down the raft, weaving in and out among the horses.

Finally, both gentlemen lay wounded and exhausted on the raft. Porthos's chest swelled with pride.

"Uh, Porthos." Aramis tapped him on the shoulder.

"What?" Porthos turned around and saw that another troop of the Cardinal's Guards now stood waiting on the far shore, their muskets aimed and their swords drawn.

"Can you swim?" Aramis asked.

"No, but I hope my horse can," Porthos replied.

"There's one way to find out." Aramis mounted his stallion, and Porthos did the same. They walked the horses to the edge of the raft and then stopped.

"You go first," Aramis said. "I'll watch your progress."

"No, no," Porthos insisted. "After you."

Finally, they grinned and nodded at each other. "One, two, *three*!"

They spurred their horses into the roaring, swirling current. The frigid water swept them downstream through twists and turns, around huge rocks, and past dangerous whirlpools. Finally, tired and chilled to the bone, the weary Musketeers and their horses staggered up onto the riverbank.

Facing them was another, even larger troop of Guards.

Porthos glanced back at the water, but a few dozen yards away the river disappeared over a waterfall. If they tried to escape again that way, they would surely be smashed on the rocks or drown. Yet, for once, even Porthos could see that the troop before them was too large to hope to defeat.

Aramis glared angrily at him. " 'A nice relaxing boat ride,' indeed."

Porthos shrugged sheepishly and pulled out his sword to face the Guards. "Good luck, Aramis," he said. "This time we're really going to need it."

## 9

MANY MILES AWAY Athos and d'Artagnan stood beside a pond while their horses drank. They were surrounded by a tall, dark forest. There was no sign of the Guards who had been pursuing them.

"Do you think we've lost them?" d'Artagnan asked.

"They'll catch up eventually," Athos said. "Are you afraid?"

"No," the younger man replied. "I would be proud to die for my king."

"There are better things to do with your life than give it away," Athos said.

"Not for a Musketeer," d'Artagnan said.

"That is a life I would save you from if I could," Athos said, shaking his head sadly. "Take some advice: Don't go looking for experience. It will find you

· 65 ·

soon enough. And when it does, it will mark you forever."

They got back on their horses and continued on their way. It wasn't long, however, before the peace was broken by the sound of hoofbeats and pistol shots. Six horsemen crashed through the woods behind them. Athos and d'Artagnan spurred their mounts up a wooded hill.

Suddenly d'Artagnan felt a searing pain as a bullet grazed his shoulder. He lost his balance and almost fell from his horse but managed to hang on. Another shot whizzed past him and struck the horse Athos was riding. The horse went down. Athos tumbled to the ground, pulled his pistol, and fired back. An approaching Guard let out a cry and fell backward off his horse. But the others kept coming.

Holding his bleeding shoulder, d'Artagnan rode up beside Athos.

"I'll hold them off as long as I can," Athos told him. "Go on without me."

"I can't leave you here," d'Artagnan protested. "Not like this." He knew Athos wouldn't stand a chance against the approaching horsemen.

"Ride to Calais and stop the cardinal's messenger," Athos said.

"But I can't leave you," d'Artagnan repeated. The next thing he knew he was staring into the muzzle of Athos's pistol.

"Go, or I'll shoot you myself!" Athos ordered.

More shots whizzed past them. Athos turned and fired back at the approaching Guards, but he was clearly outnumbered. D'Artagnan pulled out his own pistol.

"At least take this," he said, tossing it to the other man.

"Thanks," Athos said. "Now don't let us down."

D'Artagnan was suddenly choked with emotion. He was sure he would never see Athos alive again. "I'll never forget you!" he yelled.

"Just go!" Athos shouted back gruffly.

D'Artagnan turned and galloped away. The sound of shots behind him was strangely reassuring. As long as the shooting continued, it meant that Athos was still alive.

Suddenly the shots stopped. D'Artagnan pulled up his horse and listened. There was nothing but quiet. D'Artagnan shook his head sadly and urged his steed on toward Calais.

He rode all day and into the night. But fatigue and loss of blood from his wound were catching up with him. He had just passed a sign that said Calais 15 Leagues when he finally lost consciousness and tumbled off his horse to the ground.

\*　　\*　　\*

When d'Artagnan opened his eyes he was shocked to find himself in a large, comfortable bed. A fire roared in a fireplace, and a table nearby held food and wine. A beautiful woman with curly blond hair sat at the edge of the bed. As d'Artagnan's eyes focused he recognized her as the woman he'd seen in the carriage back in Paris.

"It's you," he said, his eyes widening.

"Have we met?" the woman asked.

"I saw you in Paris," d'Artagnan said. "Uh, where am I now?"

"Calais," she replied.

"Calais!" D'Artagnan jumped out of bed, then realized he was naked. He quickly grabbed a sheet and pulled it around himself. "Where are my clothes?"

"They were filthy. I'm having them washed. Is something wrong?"

"What day is it?" d'Artagnan asked. He knew that the ship the cardinal's messenger was taking was to sail Tuesday at midnight.

"It's Tuesday, near nine o'clock." The woman stood. She wore a soft blue nightgown. "Are you in a hurry to go somewhere?"

Something in her voice told d'Artagnan that she didn't want him to go. He stared around the room again. "How did I get here?"

"I found you on the road," she replied. She paused and smiled. "Do you have a name, or shall I make one up?"

"D'Artagnan." He felt his arm and realized someone had bandaged his wound.

"I like that name," she said. "I am the Countess de Winter. Milady."

"Countess?" d'Artagnan repeated, surprised.

· 68 ·

"My husband is dead," Milady said.

"I'm sorry to hear that," d'Artagnan said.

"I have learned to live with death," she said, moving closer to him and gazing into his eyes. D'Artagnan couldn't help but feel the magnetic pull of her beauty.

"Uh, I'm very grateful for what you've done," he said nervously. "But I can't stay. I've got, er, important business."

"How mysterious," Milady said with an alluring smile. "A handsome young man with important business in the middle of the night. Does it involve a young lady?"

"No."

"Does it require clothes?" Milady asked enticingly.

"Uh, yes, I need my clothes."

"Too bad," she said. "They won't be ready for at least an hour."

"An hour?" D'Artagnan swallowed. His throat felt dry and scratchy.

"I told the innkeeper to bring them when they were clean and dry," Milady said. "Until then, I'm afraid you're my prisoner. Would you care for something to drink?"

"I *am* thirsty," d'Artagnan admitted.

Milady went to the table and poured him a goblet of wine. "Let us sit by the fire and eat and drink. You can tell me how you came to lie unconscious in the middle of the night on the road to Calais." She handed him the wine. As he took it she caressed his hand with hers and smiled at him again.

\*     \*     \*

In a cold stone room in the palace, Count de Rochefort polished the sword that had once belonged to d'Artagnan. He stood up and plunged it through the candlelight. Behind him Cardinal Richelieu entered the room.

"The wonderful thing about an imaginary opponent is that he is always greatly skilled and always easily defeated," the cardinal commented wryly. "The pride of victory without the risk of loss. If only life were like that."

"Have you received any news?" Rochefort asked, sheathing his sword.

"Milady has reached Calais," Richelieu said.

Rochefort smiled. "I told you not to worry about the Musketeers. They are surely dead by now."

"Then Buckingham's signature will be on the treaty by morning," the cardinal said. "And the king's celebration will proceed as planned."

"And our plans?" Rochefort asked.

"Will proceed as well," the cardinal said with a sinister smile. He poured them each a glass of wine, then held his up for a toast. "Long live the king."

# 10

D'ARTAGNAN AND MILADY sat on a rug before the fireplace. Milady had eaten some of her food, but d'Artagnan had hardly touched his. He had no appetite. He finished his wine and stared into the flames of the fire. Milady watched him.

"You are sad," she said softly.

"I was thinking about my friends," d'Artagnan replied. "The three best friends a man could have. We were separated on our way to Calais. I'm afraid I'll never see them again."

"What brings you here?" Milady asked.

"I'd like to tell you, but I can't," d'Artagnan said slowly.

"Yes, you said it was important business," Milady said, reaching over and touching his hair. "I understand. Men make bold plans in secret. Women wait to mourn or celebrate the outcome. It's a lonely experience."

D'Artagnan felt more drawn to her than ever. "All I can tell you is that I'm on a mission for the king."

Milady laughed. "Oh, I've heard that one before."

D'Artagnan frowned. Why was she laughing? He was telling the truth. "I'm serious."

"You are a young man," Milady said. "Young men are given to exaggeration. However, if you would like to entertain me with a story, I'd be delighted to hear it."

"It's not an exaggeration," d'Artagnan insisted. "I came here to stop a traitor from sailing to England."

Milady froze for a second but recovered before d'Artagnan noticed. "A traitor, you say?"

D'Artagnan nodded. "This person carries a message of betrayal for the Duke of Buckingham."

"Aren't you afraid?" Milady asked.

"Musketeers are not afraid of anything." D'Artagnan puffed out his chest.

"I knew it," Milady said. "I knew you were a Musketeer the moment I saw you."

"You did?" The news delighted d'Artagnan. Even though he wasn't officially a Musketeer, he already felt like one.

"Of course," Milady said. She moved closer and spoke confidentially. "But d'Artagnan, if this messenger was to find out you were here, your life could be in grave danger."

"Maybe," d'Artagnan replied. When she was so

close to him, he found her very hard to resist. "But not now."

"How do you know?" Milady asked, moving even closer. "Perhaps *I'm* dangerous."

Her beauty and the intoxicating smell of her perfume overwhelmed d'Artagnan. "You're not dangerous—you're beautiful."

Milady was only inches away now. She ran her fingertip down the line of his jaw. "Beauty and danger are the same," she whispered.

The next thing d'Artagnan knew, she was kissing him gently on the lips. D'Artagnan felt almost paralyzed by her beauty. He was so entranced that he didn't notice when she reached up into her thick curls and began to draw out a pointed ivory comb. Instead, the thought of the beautiful auburn-haired woman came into his mind. *She* was the one he truly desired. Milady tried to kiss him again, but he backed away.

"No, Countess," he said. "I'm sorry."

Milady's hand with the comb flashed toward him. Because d'Artagnan had pulled back, he saw it just in time and knocked it away. Milady dove for it.

"What are you doing?" d'Artagnan gasped. "Have you lost your mind?"

"You came to Calais to stop a messenger from sailing to England," Milady said, crawling across the rug.

*She was the messenger!* The realization was like a slap in the face. D'Artagnan dove after Milady and grabbed the pointed comb. In the struggle her gown

· 73 ·

ripped at the shoulder, and d'Artagnan found himself staring at a fleur-de-lis . . . the mark of a murderess!

"My God!" d'Artagnan gasped.

"Parker!" Milady shouted.

The door burst open, and two men hurried in. The first, Parker, was the same man who'd pushed d'Artagnan off the carriage back in Paris. The other was Milady's driver, who was named Henri.

Parker stepped forward, holding out his bare hands to show that he bore no weapons. Believing in a fair fight, d'Artagnan threw Milady's comb away and, in a flash, was pummeled with kicks and blows. The next thing d'Artagnan knew, Parker was holding him while Henri approached with a dagger in his hand.

"Kill him," Milady ordered coldly.

D'Artagnan tried to squirm out of Parker's grip, but it was no use. He had to think of something fast.

"You can kill me," he told Milady. "But a surprise waits for you in England. And even Lord Buckingham can't prevent it." It was a bluff. D'Artagnan held his breath, hoping she'd fall for it.

Milady quickly raised her hand to stop Henri. Then she stepped toward d'Artagnan. "You are young, vain, and foolish. But I don't know if you are clever."

She studied his face as she tried to make up her mind. "All right, you'll go with us," she said finally. "Parker will devise ways to convince you to share your secret with me. It will be a long voyage."

A little while later Milady left the room, followed by d'Artagnan, wearing his newly washed clothes.

Henri walked beside d'Artagnan, pressing the hidden blade of his dagger against the young man's side. Parker followed close behind them.

They were about to enter the tavern when Milady gasped and stepped back into the hallway. At the bar an intense young man was holding the innkeeper by the collar and impatiently shooting questions at him.

"The back stairs," Milady hissed. "And hurry!"

Henri pushed d'Artagnan ahead. It was clear that Milady was avoiding the young man in the tavern. A few minutes later d'Artagnan was shoved into Milady's carriage. Milady and Parker joined him. Outside, Henri cracked the reins, and the carriage started to move, followed by seven more bodyguards on horseback.

In the carriage Milady seemed very pensive. D'Artagnan had a feeling he knew what she was thinking about.

"What did the man in the inn want?" he asked.

Milady shook her head. "Justice. Honor. Revenge."

"Why?" asked d'Artagnan.

"He is Armand de Winter, the brother of my late husband, Lord de Winter," Milady said. "Armand blames me for his brother's death. He thinks I murdered him."

"Did you?"

"What do *you* think?" Milady replied.

D'Artagnan stared into her lovely pale face and remembered the story Athos had told him about

· 75 ·

Count Berry. "I think he is not the first husband you've killed," he said slowly. He had just realized that Athos himself was Count Berry, and that Milady de Winter had been his beautiful young wife. Somehow she had managed to escape the executioner without Athos's knowledge.

Milady looked surprised. "What do you mean?"

"I knew a man named Count Berry once," d'Artagnan said. "He told me a story of beauty and sorrow. He was the bravest man I've ever known."

"And the saddest," Milady said, looking down at the carriage floor.

Soon they reached the harbor. It was dark, and the fog was so thick that only the masts of the schooners could be seen. The carriage rolled out onto a dock and stopped beside a ship. Henri helped Milady out, and Parker followed, holding d'Artagnan tightly.

Surrounded by the bodyguards, they walked toward a dark ship that was bobbing gently by the dock. The name on her barnacle-encrusted hull was *Persephone*. Henri stepped ahead.

"We are the Countess de Winter's party," he called toward the ship. "Asking permission to board."

"Permission granted," called a voice through the fog.

The party walked across the narrow gangplank and stepped onto the deck of the ship. A tall figure stood nearby. D'Artagnan assumed he was a member of the crew.

"Take us to your captain," Henri said.

The man neither moved nor replied.

"Are you deaf?" Henri asked.

When the man still did not reply, Henri grabbed him by the shoulder and shook him. As he did so the man pitched forward and fell with a thud against the deck. Henri and the others jumped back.

"He's dead!" Henri gasped.

"I should hope so!" a familiar voice shouted from above.

D'Artagnan looked up to see Porthos and Aramis come swinging down on ropes from the masts, kicking over several of Milady's bodyguards as they came at them. D'Artagnan stared at them with his eyes wide and his mouth agape.

"You look as if you've seen a ghost," Aramis said as he landed on the deck near him.

"Two of them," d'Artagnan managed to reply.

Meanwhile, Porthos waded through the body-guards, swinging his weapons. "All those who wish to die, please raise your hands! Don't be shy. There's plenty to go around!"

The fight began in earnest. D'Artagnan grabbed a sword and joined in. The first man he faced was Parker, who was spinning two short swords in his hands. D'Artagnan swung his own sword, but in a flash Parker knocked it high into the air. D'Artagnan heard a splash as it landed in the water beside the ship. He stared at Parker, who stepped toward him, spinning the short swords ominously. D'Artagnan looked around desperately for something with which to defend himself, but there was nothing at hand. He turned to run but fell on the slippery deck. Parker stepped closer and loomed over him. He raised his swords high over his head, an evil glint in his eye.

*"Ahh!"* Suddenly Parker's face contorted as the point of a sword burst out of his chest. The huge man fell heavily to the deck, revealing Athos behind him.

"Sorry I'm late," Athos said. "Did I miss anything?"

D'Artagnan jumped to his feet and embraced him. "I thought you were dead."

"Just keep your mind on the mission," Athos said with a wink, turning d'Artagnan around and pushing a sword into his hand. Together they dove back into the fray.

"Did you find the cardinal's messenger?" Athos yelled above the clash of swords and bursts of pistol fire.

"Yes," d'Artagnan replied.

"Did you kill him?" Athos asked.

"The messenger is a woman," d'Artagnan said. "Look!"

Athos turned and stared into the foggy shadows. There, just barely visible in the filtered moonlight, he saw Milady.

"No," he gasped in disbelief.

Milady turned and ran back across the gangplank to the dock. She jumped onto a horse and galloped away into the night. Athos leapt onto another horse and followed her.

Milady's horse raced away across the dark cobblestones of the port plaza and through the town. Her cloak slipped back, and her long blond hair flew out behind her, dancing in the night air. Athos urged his horse on, smelling the fragrant trail of perfume Milady left behind her. His feelings were a mixture of amazement that she was still alive and a rekindled sense of regret for what he'd done. He almost wanted to let her escape as a way to try to make it up to her, but for the king's sake he knew he could not.

Somewhere along the dark harbor road outside of town, Athos overtook her. He grabbed her arm, losing his balance. They both fell to the ground with a crash. In an instant Milady pulled the pointed comb from her hair and held it up, ready to plunge it into Athos's heart.

But as his eyes met hers, she paused. Then she scrambled to her feet and ran toward the dark forest.

"Stop or I'll have to shoot!" Athos shouted, pulling out his pistol.

Milady stopped and turned to face him. In the moonlight they stared at each other for the first time in fifteen years.

"How did you do it?" Athos whispered. "How did you come back from the dead?"

"A kind gentleman took pity on me," Milady replied.

"Not I," Athos said, recalling with bitterness how he'd condemned her to death.

"No, you were too proud to hear the truth," Milady said. "I learned the value of lies soon after."

Athos took a deep breath. He was one of the King's Musketeers, and he had a job to do. "Give me the cardinal's treaty."

"No."

Athos aimed the pistol. "Then I will shoot."

"Be kind," Milady whispered. "Aim for the heart."

Athos tried but found he couldn't bring himself to pull the trigger. Even after all these years, he loved her too much to try to end her life once again. Milady turned and ran right into the arms of Armand de Winter. He held the struggling woman tightly.

"Unfortunately for you," Armand said to her angrily, "I will not be so kind."

*     *     *

Later, d'Artagnan and the three Musketeers sat at a table in a Calais inn. The normally jocular men were all somber. Aramis scanned a sheet of parchment.

"The treaty outlines Richelieu's plan to forge an alliance with Buckingham," Aramis said.

"What about the king?" asked Porthos.

"He is not mentioned directly," Aramis replied as he looked over the treaty again. "But the agreement is contingent on a 'demonstration of the cardinal's power.' "

"A demonstration?" d'Artagnan asked. "What does that mean?"

Aramis shook his head. "I don't know."

Athos had been quiet all evening, but now he pushed his chair back and stood up. "I know someone who does," he said, heading for the stairway leading to the rooms on the second floor of the inn.

He climbed the stairs and knocked on a door. A moment later Armand de Winter pulled it open.

"I'd like a word with your prisoner," Athos said.

"She dies in the morning," Armand de Winter replied coldly.

Athos stepped into the room. Milady sat in a chair, staring at the fire. Near her stood a cruel-looking man in dark robes. Athos knew that Armand de Winter had hired this man to execute the prisoner when the sun rose. Athos stepped closer to Milady.

"Did you come to offer me consolation?" she asked, gazing up at him.

"No," Athos replied.

"There was a time when I would have given my life for a kind word from you," Milady said sadly.

"I know." Athos shared her sadness and spoke with regret. "I could not give it. I was a fool." He glanced at Armand de Winter, then back at Milady. "Did you kill his brother?"

Milady stared at the fire for a long time, then nodded slowly.

"Why?" Athos asked.

Milady looked surprised. "Why? Because I have become the nightmare you once thought me to be."

"Now, but not before," Athos said. "Not when we were together."

· 81 ·

"No." Milady's voice was barely a whisper. "Not when you were known as Count Berry."

Athos kneeled beside her and spoke urgently. "Do you know the cardinal's plans?"

"Yes."

"Tell me," Athos said.

"Will you spare my life?" Milady asked.

Athos glanced again at Armand de Winter, then back at her. "It's not within my power."

"Society demands swift justice," Milady said, as if recalling the past. She turned back to the fire. "I'll take the secret to my grave."

"You must die for your crimes," Athos said. "Nothing can stop that. But how you leave this world is up to you."

Milady smiled sadly and took his hand in hers. "Tell me, Count Berry, what did this world ever do for me?"

* * *

Early the next morning a melancholy procession moved along the edge of the cliffs by the sea. A hundred feet below, waves crashed on the rocky shore, and the cries of seagulls filled the air. A storm was approaching—the sky was gray, and thunder rumbled ominously in the distance. Athos led Milady, who was dressed in a plain white frock, to the edge of the cliff. Her hair was pulled back into a long braid, and she looked almost like the girl Athos had fallen in love with so long ago. Behind them walked Armand de Winter and the man in dark robes, followed by Aramis, Porthos, and d'Artagnan.

At the edge of the cliff the man in dark robes tied Milady's hands behind her back and took out a sword. Athos caught Milady's gaze and held it as Aramis delivered the last rites in a low voice.

"On your knees," said the man in dark robes. "I forgive you for your crimes. May you die in peace."

Milady sank to her knees. The man brushed her hair away from her neck and raised his sword.

"No!" Athos stepped forward and grabbed the man's wrist. He pulled Milady to her feet and held her by the shoulders. They stared into each other's eyes.

"None of this would have happened if it wasn't for me," he whispered. "Please forgive me."

"I do," Milady whispered back. He embraced her, and they kissed. Then Milady brought her lips up to his ear and whispered, "The cardinal intends to assassinate the king at his birthday celebration on Friday."

Athos stiffened. The news stunned him. It was now Wednesday morning, and they were more than two hundred leagues from Paris.

"You'll have to hurry," Milady whispered.

Athos looked back at her. "I can't let you go."

"Then the king *and* I will die."

Athos knew she spoke the truth. But how could he let her die? She was the only woman he'd ever truly loved. He glanced at Armand de Winter and the man in dark robes.

"I know what you're thinking," Milady whispered. "Don't do it. My time has come."

"No!" Athos hissed.

"Yes! Believe me, it's better this way. We could never again be what we once were."

"But—"

Without warning, Milady pushed him away. Then she turned and threw herself over the edge of the cliff.

Thunder crashed. Athos and Armand de Winter rushed to the edge of the cliff and stared down. When Athos turned back to the other Musketeers, his eyes were glistening with tears.

But when he spoke, his voice showed no sign of emotion. "We must hurry," he said. "The king's life is in danger. It is time for all the Musketeers to be called back into service."

# 11

WHILE D'ARTAGNAN and the three Musketeers were riding as fast as they could back to Paris, Cardinal Richelieu and Count de Rochefort were standing in a field just outside the city limits. Near them a life-size portrait of King Louis leaned against a tree.

Bang! A shot rang out, and the painting tipped over and fell. Rochefort stepped forward and picked it up. Wisps of smoke rose from a bullet hole directly over the king's heart. As Richelieu joined him, the count looked across the field at a solitary marksman far away.

"Most impressive," Cardinal Richelieu said.

"He can do it every time," said Rochefort.

"And he has no qualms about what you've asked him to do?" Richelieu asked.

"None," replied Rochefort. "He believes that man should honor no kings before God."

"A man of faith," Richelieu said with a bemused smile. "How delightful. Whatever you're paying him, double it. I want the king's birthday to be a memorable event. And rehang this painting in my chamber."

"But what about the bullet hole?" Rochefort asked.

"I want it to hang just the way it is," Richelieu replied.

\* \* \*

D'Artagnan and the three Musketeers rode hard with their blue-and-gold tunics revealed for all to see. As Wednesday passed into Thursday, their pace hardly slowed. In village after village they were met with cheers and they scattered sheets of parchment printed with the slogan All for One and One for All! Throughout the countryside the word was passed. And throughout the countryside Musketeers threw down their rakes and hoes and picked up their swords.

## 12

FRIDAY WAS A GLORIOUS, sunny day. A festive mood filled the air as the citizens of Paris crowded the streets on their way to the palace. Today was the king's birthday, and everyone had been invited to attend.

Inside the palace, the halls were filled with noblemen and ladies dressed in their finest. King Louis and Queen Anne were in the throne room. In a few moments they would step through the open doors onto the balcony and greet the citizens of France.

Amid the noise and preparations, the young king and queen stood quietly side by side.

"Anne?" Louis said in a low, nervous voice.

"Yes?" Anne looked hopefully into his eyes.

"I have often wished to speak with you," he said. "Not as king to queen but as husband to wife."

Queen Anne wasn't sure how to reply. She had

· 87 ·

waited months for this and had almost given up hope. She glanced over the king's shoulder and saw Constance in the background, smiling hopefully for her.

"You look beautiful," the king said.

"Thank you," Anne replied with a shy smile. They stepped toward the balcony. From outside came the sounds of the thousands of waiting subjects. Anne seemed to hesitate.

"Are you afraid?" Louis whispered.

"Yes," replied Anne.

"It's not so hard," Louis said. "We simply stand and wave."

"I wasn't speaking of *this*," Anne replied.

"Then what?"

Anne glanced at him. Even though they'd been married for several months, she still didn't know him very well, and she knew that what she wanted to tell him would be terribly shocking. "You would not believe me."

"A husband should believe his wife in all things," Louis replied, looking thoughtful and sincere.

"Love before belief," Anne replied.

King Louis moved closer and slid his hand into hers. "Tell me your secret and I will prove myself worthy . . . of both."

Anne looked up into his eyes and saw for the first time the beginnings of the love she had prayed for. She squeezed his hand, and together they moved toward the balcony and the crowd below.

· 88 ·

\*     \*     \*

Across the room Cardinal Richelieu stood with Count de Rochefort, watching the young king and queen.

"I'm not sure which is sadder," Richelieu muttered. "To die so young, or to die a king."

"France will not go wanting," Rochefort replied. "A new king will sit on the throne. A true king, after all."

Richelieu smiled at the thought of himself seated on the throne. "Are you sure everything is ready?"

"I'd stake my life on it," Rochefort replied.

"Rest assured," the cardinal said with a dark smile. "You have."

\*     \*     \*

The streets of Paris were so crowded with people that d'Artagnan and the three Musketeers were forced to dismount and continue on foot. In the distance they could see the castle and the festively draped balcony from which the king would soon greet the people. Guarding the palace was a double line of the Cardinal's Guards in their crimson-and-gold tunics.

"It'll take an army to get through those guards," Porthos grumbled as they pushed their way through the crowd.

Athos turned to d'Artagnan. "Look through the surrounding area," he ordered. "We'll try to reach the king."

"But . . ." D'Artagnan didn't want to be left behind.

"Go!" Athos shouted.

· 89 ·

Disappointed, d'Artagnan stopped and looked up at the surrounding buildings. How was he supposed to find out anything out here? Suddenly he saw a glint of sunlight reflected off a musket barrel high on the roof of a building across the square. D'Artagnan quickly turned to tell the Musketeers, but it was too late. They'd already disappeared into the crowd.

D'Artagnan looked up again. A marksman on the roof across from the palace could mean only one thing. D'Artagnan started to run. He'd have to take care of this on his own.

*   *   *

In the throne room, only a few feet from the balcony, Anne suddenly stopped. King Louis gave her a questioning glance.

"I want to tell you my secret now," she said.

"Yes?" The king's eyebrows rose.

"Cardinal Richelieu . . . is an evil man," Anne whispered.

"Do not believe everything you hear," the king replied automatically. "He is powerful and therefore is the target of rumors."

"I ride through the countryside every day," Anne said. "I have seen the uses of his power."

"Power sometimes frightens," King Louis replied.

"I have seen it here in the palace," Anne cautioned. "*And* in my own chambers."

King Louis stared at her. "What do you mean?"

Anne took a deep breath and let it out slowly. "The

cardinal has made it clear that he wants me for himself."

King Louis was quiet for a moment as he considered what his wife had just told him. Then he nodded. "I believe you," he replied.

"What will we do?" Anne asked.

"I'm not sure," King Louis said, squeezing her hand. "But we will do it together."

\* \* \*

D'Artagnan raced up the stairway two steps at a time. There was no telling exactly when the king and queen would step out onto the balcony, but it would certainly be soon. D'Artagnan's legs ached from the strain as he raced up staircase after staircase.

Suddenly through an open window came the sound of blaring trumpets. The king was about to appear before the people! D'Artagnan hurled himself upward even faster.

He reached a door and threw himself through it, bursting onto the slanted roof of the building. The sun was bright, and it made him squint. A dozen feet away he could see the marksman crouching and carefully aiming a musket at the balcony across the square. The marksman's finger was closing on the trigger.

D'Artagnan dove at him.

Bang! A shot rang out.

The next thing d'Artagnan knew, he and the marksman were sliding down the pitched roof of the building. The edge was coming up fast. And after

· 91 ·

that only empty air would lie between them and the cobblestoned courtyard nearly eighty feet below.

*    *    *

The rifle shot had missed the king by inches, crashing into the wall behind him. In the stunned moment that followed, Louis turned and saw anger and disappointment in Cardinal Richelieu's eyes.

Richelieu moved quickly past the king to the balcony's edge. In the square below he saw the huge crowd begin to panic at the sound of the gunshot. Three men in blue-and-gold tunics emerged from the crowd, trying to force their way into the palace.

Richelieu thought fast. "Kill them!" he shouted at his guards. "The Musketeers are trying to assassinate the king!"

"Wait!" King Louis began. But Richelieu turned to the Guards around him.

"Get the king and queen inside," he ordered. Despite their protests, Louis and Anne were quickly ushered away.

In the square below, Porthos, Aramis, and Athos drew their swords and prepared to take on the dozens of Cardinal's Guards who stood between them and the palace. The task seemed impossible, and the Guards looked upon the three men with amusement.

But their smug looks changed to astonishment as Musketeers began to appear from every corner of the square, throwing off their disguises to reveal their blue-and-gold tunics. With well-trained precision, the Musketeers lined up behind Athos, Porthos, and Ar-

· 92 ·

amis. They raised their swords, and a hundred blades flashed in the sunlight.

"Save the king!" Athos shouted as he led the Musketeers into battle.

\*     \*     \*

High above the fighting, d'Artagnan and the marksman dangled precariously from the edge of the roof. As d'Artagnan began to pull himself back up, he glanced at the marksman, who was hanging a few feet away. To d'Artagnan's amazement the marksman let go of the edge with one hand and pulled out his sword.

"Are you insane?" d'Artagnan gasped.

The marksman answered by jabbing the sword at him. D'Artagnan barely managed to swing out of the way. Porthos's words rang in his ears. *There's one rule: Stay alive.* D'Artagnan pulled out his own sword and, hanging by one hand, began to duel.

\*     \*     \*

In the square, the battle between the Musketeers and the Cardinal's Guards was in full swing. Aramis skewered Guards with his usual precision. Porthos dispatched them with his extensive collection of bizarre weapons.

Athos was busy cutting a swath through the group of Guards in front of him when Porthos grabbed his arm and pointed upward.

"Look!" Porthos yelled. "Our young friend likes to live life on the edge!"

They watched as d'Artagnan and the marksman,

· 93 ·

still hanging from the edge of the roof, exchanged blows.

"I believe d'Artagnan could use some help," Athos said.

"Coming right up," Porthos replied, pulling a crossbow out of his cape. He fired, and its arrow struck the marksman squarely in the back. The marksman let out a scream and plunged to the ground.

D'Artagnan waved down at his friends. "It's about time!" he shouted.

"Quit hanging around," Porthos shouted back. "We have a king to save."

*     *     *

Richelieu's Guards escorted the king and queen into the throne room. One of the Guards locked the large wooden door leading to the great hall. Constance was brought into the throne room through another door and held by a Guard. Finally, King Louis managed to tear himself away from the Guards and confront Cardinal Richelieu.

"Your plan has failed," the king said.

"You are mistaken," Cardinal Richelieu replied. "This couldn't be more perfect. The king of France dies at the hands of his own personal guards. The country is in chaos at the loss of its leader."

BOOM! Something slammed into the tall wooden door. Realizing that someone was trying to break it down and get in, Richelieu turned to his Guards.

"Secure that door!" he ordered, and a dozen

Guards pressed themselves against the door. Richelieu stepped to the throne and sat down.

"The power behind the throne steps forward," he said triumphantly, "and now sits on the throne. A man of God. A man of the people."

BOOM! The door bent and creaked under the strain.

"You will have to kill me first," King Louis said to the cardinal.

"That is precisely the idea," Richelieu replied. Turning to Rochefort, he pointed at the king and queen. "Kill him. And her, too."

Rochefort drew d'Artagnan's sword and advanced toward Louis and Anne. Louis drew his own sword, trying not to tremble. He knew he was no match for the captain of the Cardinal's Guards.

BOOM! CRASH! The door to the great hall burst open, sending the Guards in front of it flying. Dozens of Musketeers charged in, led by Athos, Porthos, and Aramis.

"Greetings!" Athos shouted at Count de Rochefort. "Are we interrupting?"

"On the contrary, you are right on time." Rochefort turned his sword toward Athos, and they began to duel.

Within seconds a full-fledged battle was raging in the throne room. A group of Musketeers tried to protect Louis and Anne, but the young king insisted on joining the fight. Even Anne found a way to help—when one of the Cardinal's Guards tried to sneak behind a curtain to grab her, she ran a sword through him.

In the midst of the fray the duel between Athos and Rochefort gained intensity as the two men jabbed and parried across the room. Suddenly Rochefort spun around and slashed Athos across the arm. Athos staggered back, clutching his wounded arm. Rochefort had a nasty sneer on his face as he moved forward to finish the Musketeer off.

Just as Rochefort was about to deliver the fatal blow, however, Athos suddenly switched sword hands and began to fight back. Their swords clashed in a stalemate. Looking for an advantage, Rochefort reached to his belt and pulled out a dagger. Athos stepped forward and smashed the count in the face with his fist.

Rochefort went sprawling. His sword slid across the room until someone's foot stopped it. Rochefort crawled after it and looked up to find d'Artagnan standing on the blade.

"Excuse me," d'Artagnan said, picking up the sword. "I believe this belongs to me."

While the battle continued on all sides, Cardinal Richelieu quietly stepped behind King Louis and held a small pistol to his head. Louis dropped his sword.

"The throne will be mine," Richelieu hissed. He turned to some nearby Guards. "Get the queen."

The Guards grabbed the queen and began to drag her away.

"They have the king!" Constance cried.

Richelieu and the Guards pushed the struggling king and queen to a wall, which opened to reveal a secret passage. They quickly started down it.

"Porthos! Aramis!" Athos shouted as he ran after them. The two Musketeers followed him, leaving d'Artagnan to face Count de Rochefort alone.

"Let's discover if you are as brave a man as your father," Rochefort said as their blades clashed. "And as foolish."

"You were there when he died," d'Artagnan said.

"He died for his king and for France," Rochefort replied. "But most of all, he died at the end of my sword."

D'Artagnan was so stunned he almost stopped fighting. "You killed my father?"

"As I will kill you," Rochefort replied, attacking the young man furiously.

D'Artagnan used every trick he knew to counter Rochefort's slashing sword. Suddenly Rochefort caught him by the shoulder and threw him against the hard stone wall. D'Artagnan's head banged against the wall, and he was momentarily stunned.

"How pathetic," Rochefort hissed. "To be killed by the same man who killed your father."

But d'Artagnan wasn't beaten yet. He ducked and kicked Rochefort in the stomach. The sword fight continued down a long staircase until Rochefort grabbed a candle from the wall and threw it into d'Artagnan's face. Blinded by the hot wax, d'Artagnan lost his sword, which clattered down the stairs.

"Prepare to join your father!" Rochefort shouted, lunging forward.

D'Artagnan leapt up in the air and did a flip over the count's head. He landed next to his sword and picked it up.

"Impressive," Rochefort had to admit.

"You'll find that I'm full of surprises," d'Artagnan replied with a smile.

# 13

THE THREE MUSKETEERS hurried down the dimly lit passage in the direction Richelieu and the others had gone, but they'd lost sight of them. The Musketeers didn't know it, but Richelieu and his Guards had already led the king and queen through a series of passages leading into the caverns beneath the Bastille.

"Are you all right?" Louis asked Anne as they were shoved along by the Guards.

"As long as I'm with you," she whispered back.

"Such a touching sentiment," Richelieu said with a sneer. "Too bad you'll only take it with you to your graves."

\* \* \*

Somewhere in the dark behind them the three Musketeers also reached the Bastille. They stopped at an intersection of three tunnels leading off in different directions. Torches cast eerie shadows against the stone walls around them, and they could hear prisoners' cries in the distance.

"Which tunnel shall we take?" Aramis asked.

"Don't ask me," Porthos replied. "I've never been here before."

"Split up," Athos ordered curtly.

\* \* \*

D'Artagnan and Rochefort fought down another shadowy flight of stairs. Suddenly d'Artagnan slipped and fell to the bottom. He dropped his sword, and it clattered away into the darkness. He tried to get to his feet but lost his balance and fell again.

Above him Rochefort laughed and started down the stairs, taking his time. D'Artagnan knew he was finished. He was too dizzy to stand, and his sword had fallen well out of his reach.

"D'Artagnan," a voice whispered from the shadows.

D'Artagnan's eyes widened. He'd recognize that voice anywhere—it belonged to the beautiful auburn-haired woman! A second later he felt the handle of his sword slide into his hand.

"Thank you," d'Artagnan whispered. "But what are you doing here?"

"Making sure you win," Constance whispered back.

Meanwhile, Rochefort loomed over him. "One thing is for certain," the count said with a cruel laugh. "You're no Musketeer."

Rochefort raised his sword to stab d'Artagnan. In a flash d'Artagnan rolled over and lunged, plunging his sword into the count's chest.

"That was for my father," d'Artagnan muttered as Rochefort crumbled to the floor before him, dead.

*     *     *

Deep beneath the Bastille, Richelieu and his Guards led the king and queen to a small boat waiting at a stone dock in a misty underground cavern. A lone hooded figure waited to steer the boat away. The Guards were just getting the king and queen onto the boat when Athos raced around the corner.

"Kill him!" Richelieu shouted. Several of the Guards turned and began to fight with Athos. But a second later Porthos joined him, his sword drawn.

The two of them disposed of the Guards quickly. But by then the boat had moved a safe distance away from the stone dock.

"You're too late, Musketeers!" Richelieu shouted. "By now the Duke of Buckingham's signature is next to mine on the treaty. The alliance is complete!"

"That would be difficult," Athos replied, pulling the treaty out of his tunic, "considering the treaty never left France."

The cardinal looked stunned, but he quickly regained his composure. "A minor problem. The king and queen will soon be dead. The throne will still be mine."

"Not if I have anything to do with it," the hooded figure in the boat said, throwing off his hood.

· 101 ·

"Aramis!" Richelieu gasped.

"You will never harm another man or woman again," Aramis said. "That is my promise to God." He raised his sword to strike Richelieu down. But suddenly King Louis stepped between them and turned to Richelieu.

"This is a complicated matter, affecting both France and the crown," the king said. "Until my advisers and I can determine the whole truth, Cardinal, I invite you to enjoy the comforts of the Bastille."

With that, the king smashed his fist into Cardinal Richelieu's face, knocking him out of the boat and into the water.

"I hope you find your new home pleasant," the king said.

"Well done, Your Majesty." Aramis patted him on the shoulder.

Anne rushed into the king's arms and gave him a long, deep kiss.

"The king could be a Musketeer!" Porthos exclaimed with admiration.

## 14

THE FOLLOWING DAY a special ceremony was held in the throne room. Musketeers lined a red-carpeted walkway leading to King Louis and Queen Anne on their throne. Athos, Aramis, Porthos, and d'Artagnan walked proudly along the red carpet toward the royal couple.

"Is this the young man who saved my life?" Louis asked, smiling down at d'Artagnan.

"His name is d'Artagnan," Porthos said, placing his hand proudly on his young friend's shoulder.

"Approach, d'Artagnan," the king commanded.

His heart pounding nervously, d'Artagnan stepped toward the king and queen. Suddenly he remembered something. Reaching into his jacket, he took out the thin gold bracelet he had found on the road.

"I have something that belongs to you, Your Majesty," he said, offering the bracelet to Queen Anne.

"Thank you, d'Artagnan," the queen replied. "But it is not mine. I believe it belongs to Constance."

D'Artagnan turned and found himself face-to-face with the auburn-haired woman. With his heart beating even harder, he slipped the bracelet around her wrist.

"So your name is Constance," he said.

"Yes." Constance thanked him with a kiss on the cheek.

"D'Artagnan, I am in your debt," the king said. "What can I do to repay the courage you've shown me? Name anything, and it will be yours."

D'Artagnan gulped. He knew exactly what he wanted to say, but he was so nervous and tongue-tied that he couldn't get the words out.

"His heart has only one desire, Your Majesty," Athos answered for him. "To become a Musketeer."

D'Artagnan nodded eagerly.

"Then kneel," the king said.

D'Artagnan dropped to his knees, and the king laid the blade of his sword on each of his shoulders in turn.

"The world is an uncertain realm, filled with danger," the king said. "Truth despoiled by broken promises. Honor undermined by the pursuit of gold. Freedom sacrificed when the weak are oppressed by the strong. But there are those who oppose these powerful forces, who dedicate their lives to truth, honor, and freedom. They are a constant reminder to all of us that such a life is not just possible but necessary to our continued survival. These men are known as the Musketeers. Rise and join them, d'Artagnan. You are now a Musketeer."

D'Artagnan rose with a proud smile on his face. Bells rang in the distance. Constance smiled brightly, her eyes gleaming with tears of joy as Athos presented d'Artagnan with a blue-and-gold tunic of his own. D'Artagnan hugged his three best friends. This was the happiest moment of his life.

\*　　\*　　\*

Later, the four Musketeers walked confidently down a Paris boulevard.

"I know this may sound like a stupid question," d'Artagnan said, "but what exactly does a Musketeer do?"

Porthos and Aramis exchanged a puzzled glance.

"Weren't you listening?" Porthos asked.

"We protect the king," said Athos.

"And the queen," added Porthos.

"In the name of God and France," said Aramis.

"Yes, but—" d'Artagnan began. He was suddenly interrupted by the sound of someone angrily shouting his name. He and his friends turned to see Girard standing behind them with his five brothers, their swords drawn. Girard was still covered with bandages.

"I believe we have some unfinished business," Girard said.

"Who are they?" Athos asked.

"Nuisances," said d'Artagnan.

"My sister's honor will not wait one moment more!" Girard shouted angrily.

Porthos looked over at d'Artagnan and grinned. "I *knew* he was a natural."

"They need to be taught some manners," Aramis said.

"For God and country," added Porthos.

"No." D'Artagnan shook his head firmly. "This is not your affair. I will take care of them."

D'Artagnan started toward Girard and his brothers, but Athos put his hand on the young man's shoulder and stopped him.

"Nonsense," Athos said, drawing his sword and pointing it toward the sky. "All for one . . ."

The others quickly drew their swords and raised them as well, shouting, ". . . and one for all!"

## About the Author

Todd Strasser has written many award-winning novels for young and teenage readers. He has written *The Villains Collection* and novelizations of *Honey, I Blew Up the Kid* and *Hocus Pocus* for Disney Press. He is a frequent guest at middle schools and high schools, where he speaks about writing and conducts writing workshops. He and his wife and children live in Westchester County, New York.